THE REVENGE OF COLONEL BLOOD

THE REVENGE OF COLONEL BLOOD

A Four Ravens Adventure

MARK JACKSON

Copyright © 2013 Mark Jackson

The moral right of the author has been asserted.

Apart from any fair dealing for the purposes of research or private study, or criticism or review, as permitted under the Copyright, Designs and Patents Act 1988, this publication may only be reproduced, stored or transmitted, in any form or by any means, with the prior permission in writing of the publishers, or in the case of reprographic reproduction in accordance with the terms of licences issued by the Copyright Licensing Agency. Enquiries concerning reproduction outside those terms should be sent to the publishers.

Matador
9 Priory Business Park,
Wistow Road, Kibworth Beauchamp,
Leicestershire. LE8 0RX
Tel: (+44) 116 279 2299
Fax: (+44) 116 279 2277
Email: books@troubador.co.uk
Web: www.troubador.co.uk/matador

ISBN 978 1780884 684

British Library Cataloguing in Publication Data.
A catalogue record for this book is available from the British Library.

Typeset by Troubador Publishing Ltd, Leicester, UK

Matador is an imprint of Troubador Publishing Ltd

Printed and bound in the UK by TJ International, Padstow, Cornwall

For Ozzie and Matthew.

Mac's Enfield

Prologue

Ladysmith, South Africa, 1899

The Veldt seemed endless. Rock and bare earth punctuated by few stunted shrubs bent over against the heat.

Two young Gordon Highlanders were squatting in a shallow dugout.

One of the soldiers shifted his position to avoid the onset of cramp. His movements were minimal, to save his energy in the relentless sun. He patted his rifle, shifting it to match his new position. Etched on the butt of his Lee-Enfield were three letters 'Mac'.

Sergeant John 'Mac' McDonald and Lance Corporal Alistair Robertson crouched with burnt, dusty faces, stained khaki jackets and matted kilts.

Their regiment was more than 100 years old and had fought across the world in the Peninsular War, with Wellington at Waterloo and, more recently, in Afghanistan and Egypt. McDonald and Robertson had both seen action in the inhospitable Afghan mountain ranges.

The angry African sun burned down on them. Dry, hot, sapping. It drained the energy from their bodies. The only answer was to stay still and conserve their strength. They had picked their position well, overlooking a wide expanse that rose to a distant ridge.

The friends had joined up within months of each other, taking the Queen's Shilling to serve and see the world.

The British Empire spanned the globe, stretching from London, through Africa, Asia to Australia. British soldiers, drawn from England, Ireland, Scotland and Wales, manned outposts in far-flung islands and deserts. These men had signed up to fight for Queen Victoria, taken her shilling to leave their native land and serve all over the world.

McDonald was the taller of the two, raw boned, shoulders built to carry heavy loads. Robertson the stockier, his smile marred by missing teeth.

McDonald looked up at the birds circling above a ridge they were studying across the shallow valley. He took a precious swig from his canteen. He shook it gently. Still more than half full. That was good. Although he wanted to drink more, he had to take it sparingly. To run out would mean a slow death under the merciless sun. He screwed the cap back on the canteen, an uneasy feeling between his shoulder blades. His eyes fixed on the horizon.

They had been there since daybreak, assigned remote guard duty, scouts for the brigade.

Suddenly, a horseman appeared over the ridge. The rider, a gaunt figure, reined the horse back and looked over his shoulder. His torn ragged uniform was that of a British soldier. His demeanour determined, his face desperate. He wheeled the horse around and urged it forward.

McDonald shifted his position and pulled his field binoculars to his eyes.

Tight on the horseman's tail were two more riders.

Through the binoculars, the two riders looked to be closing on the desperate horseman. The hunters were Boers, South Africans, who were at war with the British. They spoke Afrikaans, a language similar to Dutch, as many had originated in Holland. They had moved to the southern tip of Africa, the great continent, to make a new life. They were a tough breed, excellent horsemen and deadly marksmen.

McDonald laid the spyglass down with deliberate care.

"Faster, man," muttered the young soldier, as he fixed on the chasing Boer riders.

The Boers closed on the exhausted rider. The leading Boer drew level with the doomed British soldier.

"Damn," McDonald's breath was quick.

The leading Boer horseman reached across to take the reins of his prey's horse. A wild grin on his face as he clasped the leather straps.

A crack echoed across the low scrub. A crimson mark spoiled the Boer's buff jacket. The Boer's face twisted as the retort of a rifle faded across the Veldt.

The Boer, open-eyed, hit the ground.

McDonald eased the trigger of his Lee-Enfield rifle and the second Boer horseman fell.

The British officer checked and looked across towards the two highlanders.

"Over here, sir. Hurry!" Robertson urged the rider. Robertson stood, waving his arms, as McDonald kept his rifle trained on the ridge.

The officer raised an arm and spurred his horse towards the two Gordon Highlanders.

The haunted strained face of Major Magnus Laird stared down at the two Gordons.

"Eh? Who are you with?" demanded the Major in crisp Scottish tones.

The two foot soldiers hastily saluted.

"Sergeant McDonald. Lance Corporal Robertson of the Gordons, sir."

The Gordon Highlanders were also known as the 92nd Regiment of Foot.

"Point for the brigade, sir," McDonald barked out the reply, eyes straight ahead. Robertson cast an eye at the ridge.

"An entire brigade? I must speak with your CO," the

young officer was obviously relieved, gracing the pair with a swift salute.

McDonald and Robertson watched as Major Laird spurred his horse away. Robertson gave his Sergeant a nudge:

"Reckon he owes you one, Mac. There'll be tin in it for you." Robertson used the army slang for a medal.

"One of Scotland's finest, Robbo. Major Magnus Laird. My father kent him," said Mac, falling back into their Scots tongue.

Robertson was distracted.

"NO!" The corporal was already snatching up his rifle.

Boer horsemen were streaming over the far ridge, waves of khaki bearing down on them. McDonald strained his eyes in the fading light.

"Now, we're cooked," he said, as he checked his weapon.

A shot rang out. Robertson crumpled. McDonald raised his rifle and fired back. He bent down, but Robertson was dead.

"Here, McDonald. Hurry man," Laird's voice was used to command.

McDonald swung around. Laird was reaching down for him. The officer hauled McDonald on to the back of his saddle and kicked his mount forward.

McDonald looked back as the Boers overran Robertson's sprawled body.

A parade was drawn up in the dawn chill. Any later in the day and standing for so long would have become unbearable. People think of Africa as a hot continent, but at night the temperature can plummet dramatically.

McDonald stepped forward as the piper struck up a slow lament. Overhead, the Union Jack and the Gordon's Regimental Colours, marking the battles the Gordon Highlanders had fought in, were barely catching the weak arid breeze. They hung limp.

A senior officer and his adjutant took a step forward and Colonel Fraser, a rotund, florid man with a heavy gait, lifted a medal out of the box offered by the junior officer.

He pinned it to McDonald's chest. McDonald looked across the camp. Major Laird was standing across the compound in front of a row of weathered tents. Laird moved his cane to his peak in recognition of the man who saved his life, before he had returned the favour. McDonald looked down as the ribbon was pinned to his chest. The Colonel placed a sympathetic hand on McDonald's shoulder.

"Pity about Robertson. Good man."

McDonald nodded, the image of Robbo's toothy smile replaced in his memory by his friend's body lying face down in the dust as Laird's horse bore him to safety.

"Yes, sir. They came on us quickly, sir."

"Quite. Right on Laird's tail," muttered the officer.

They saluted each other.

Major Laird watched McDonald intensely. McDonald stared straight ahead, the medal and ribbon bright on his breast.

LONDON, ENGLAND, 1925

Chapter 1

The Tower

The last, long rays of the day bathed the Tower of London in a natural gold wash.

McDonald followed his shadow across the stone flagged courtyard heading towards the Jewel Tower.

He passed the majestic centrepiece, the White Tower, a medieval skyscraper built by William the Conqueror, which had dominated the Thames's skyline since 1078.

The Tower had grown since then, housing through the centuries the royal mint, an armoury and the Crown Jewels.

Dusk was always the best time to see them, to appreciate the jewels' magnificence. McDonald did not consider their value, not in money. Their worth was in their beauty and, he had to acknowledge, what the treasures symbolised – the power and might of the British Empire.

McDonald paused to enjoy the evening glow. His walk to the Jewel Tower was a short one. Each step was to be savoured. The ravens were still out, chattering and arguing. It was their nature. He smiled, he would attend to them later. One duty at a time. As Ravenmaster, they were his special responsibility.

The promotion to Ravenmaster had delighted him. He felt a strange bond with the ferocious, daring birds, who strutted around the Tower as if they owned it. In a way, they did. Ravens had been at the Tower since William the Conqueror had overseen its initial construction.

The fortress, its armoury and treasure trove had grown over the centuries since 1078, as kings and queens had built additional towers, walls and moats. The Ravens had been here throughout.

Their presence was considered vital. The legend was that should the ravens ever forsake the Tower, it would fall. While they stayed, the Tower would remain.

McDonald did not think of himself as a superstitious man, yet he did not question the myth. It was part of the Tower's history, weaved into its very fabric and he took his role seriously.

He weighed the heavy bunch of keys in his hand.

John Cameron McDonald was tall and rugged, a bearded man with a glint in his eye.

The last group of tourists was being ushered out of the Jewel Tower. One figure lingered. His black-gloved hands turned a walking cane with a silver wolf's head at its crown. He leaned in closer, his breath clouding the glass. The Crown Jewels sat inches away on the other side of the pane.

A glittering array: cushioned on velvet, encased in glass, surrounded by stone walls that had shielded them for centuries.

They were worth a king's ransom, collected, gifted or stolen over the centuries. Amassed in the greatest collection of priceless treasures in the world. A symbol of the fading Empire, its majesty and glory, that underpinned Britain and its monarchy.

The figure, in a long black frock coat, breathed deeply, as his eyes devoured the linked gems.

McDonald paused as the ravens rose screeching, their cries echoing around the ancient fortress.

McDonald tensed and looked upwards at the birds circling in the eerie dusk.

The sound of different birds, the carrion of another continent came to him.

McDonald could smell it; he was back in the Veldt. McDonald looked down. His hand had involuntarily gone to his row of medals. He fingered the one he received that day. The day his friend Robertson died in the dust outside Ladysmith. Now the ribbon was simply one of many he had earned since then. He took a deep breath, remembering he had another duty to perform.

The sunset had deepened. A yeoman warder and a guardsman pulled closed the heavy oaken doors. Another warder stood watching as the Jewel House was closed for the night.

Hands tucked behind his back, he too was holding a bunch of ancient, long heavy keys. McDonald nodded to his fellow warders and turned towards the ravens' cage, sitting in the shadow of the Wakefield Tower.

McDonald's voice was gentle, coaxing:

"Come on, your highness. Don't be a prude," his tone was that of an indulgent grandfather.

McDonald made a tutting noise. He held up a thin wafer. An offering.

"Come on, your majesty. Show a little decorum," gently reproving.

The dark, gleaming, ruthless eye of a raven stared back at him.

The next day, the Tower was open for business. Early morning arrivals wandered through the main gate. McDonald was addressing a party of tourists in the courtyard. The schoolchildren were standing almost to attention in front of the towering yeoman warder.

As well as helping to guard the Tower of London, the warders also served as guides, giving talks and tours.

There was a rhythm to McDonald's storytelling:

"The Tower has had its fair share of colourful characters over the centuries. Now, I'm going to tell you the tale of a true rogue. The only man to ever succeed in stealing the Crown Jewels, Colonel Blood," McDonald lowered his voice as he uttered the name.

Like many of his fellow warders, McDonald had a soft spot for Colonel Blood. It was one of his favourite tales from the Tower's colourful, and at times, bloody, history. Thomas Blood was a daring Irishman, who along with his gang, had tried to steal the Crown Jewels in 1671. Bizarrely, his punishment had been a pardon from King Charles II and royal favour.

McDonald cleared his throat for effect.

"Colonel Blood," he started again, his eyes raking the faces of his young audience.

One of the young schoolchildren mouthed the name in awe.

★ ★ ★

In another part of London, a Hackney carriage drew up outside the Natural History Museum on Cromwell Road. Running parallel to it was Exhibition Road, which was also home to the Science Museum and the Victoria and Albert Museum. But the fare had been quite clear, the Natural History Museum and he had requested the main entrance.

The carriage door opened and a gentleman's cane emerged. The owner followed, dark sharp trousers and shiny polished shoes. He straightened his cuffs with precision.

The gentleman walked up the wide stone steps with a brisk strong walk, the cane swinging with authority.

At the entrance to the magnificent building, a doorman doffed his hat to the visitor.

The gentleman strode down the high majestic hall towards the dinosaur room.

The cane made a sharp clicking noise on the marble floor. A group of schoolchildren were clustered around an exhibit: a huge skeleton. One of the children looked around at the tapping noise. An attendant busy polishing a brass plaque looked up. Slight recognition washed over his features, before he hurriedly looked away.

The gentleman paused in front of a huge dinosaur skeleton. He was wearing smart leather gloves. He pulled them off and stood with his hands behind his back, his cane horizontal. Its crest was a silver wolf's head.

He altered his posture and the cane was placed between his shiny toecaps. Another pair of feet moved to stand beside him. The skeleton's plaque was solid brass, 'Tyrannosaurus Rex' carved into it.

"God save your king." The voice was edged, a rough Afrikaner growl. The voice of a Boer, a white African.

Dutch settlers had made the Cape, the southernmost tip of Africa, their own. The arrival of the British had forced them inland to the Transvaal and led to two bitter wars.

The voice belonged to Kruger, a good-looking athletic man in his prime. Kruger was dressed simply, nothing to mark him out apart from his face. Kruger bore a long ugly scar that ran down his tanned features.

"At your service," the tanned man inclined his head in mock deference.

★ ★ ★

Strong hands polished a pair of sturdy black army boots. Yeoman Warder Tommy Battle was concentrating on his task. A robust, good-humoured Londoner with long sideburns, he whistled as he worked. The tune *Greensleeves* was reputed to have been written by King Henry VIII.

Battle's warder's coat was hanging behind him. The only colour in a simple room. It was a soldier's billet.

Ged Keilty, a trim, thin-faced, dark-haired Irishman, was lounging in an armchair, reading a newspaper.

Battle moved on to trimming his whiskers. Absorbed in the detail of his task, he was meticulous.

Battle was eyeing the mirror. He had no need to puff his chest out. Tommy Battle could have had a tank named after him. His battered nose marked him out as a fist-fighter.

"You're an 'ansome devil," he said to the image.

Keilty looked up momentarily and shook his head ruefully.

Tourists were leaving the Tower. A young couple walked past a guardsman standing in his pillar box. A pair of yeoman warders were gently and courteously ushering people out. Standing, half hidden in an arched doorway, was McDonald. From the shadows, he watched the couple walk past.

The couple looked around for their son. The father motioned for him to hurry.

"Come along now, Harry, stop loitering."

The boy stopped a few feet in front of the guardsman. He cocked his fingers as though he had a gun and fired. The guardsman blinked. The boy turned sharply. McDonald watched him. The boy wilted and hurried after his parents. McDonald was still watching. Other tourists passed under the arch. McDonald watched the boy join his parents. McDonald nodded to the other warders and the guardsman and turned away from the heavy gate as it was slowly pushed closed to the world.

McDonald gently held a raven, examining its wing. He soothed the black bird.

"Nothing broken, lass. Just a wee knock. You'll be right as rain."

McDonald carefully put the bird back into the large black cage. The ravens were powerfully built members of the crow family. Everything about them was black.

He released the bird. It stepped away from him and glared back. McDonald laughed softly, a rough warm sound that echoed slightly around the courtyard. He pulled out a set of old long keys and locked the cage. The bird cried out at him.

"I'll call in on you later, lass."

He stepped away and pulled out a pipe. He knocked it out on the cage. Resting his tobacco box on the wall, he filled his pipe. McDonald looked up at the fortifications surrounding him. Beyond them was another castle wall. The River Thames protected the Tower's southside, a deep trench and further stone work, the ancient Keep's north face.

A rich yeoman's uniform was being brushed with extreme care. Battle examined a minor loose thread closely. A warder's red and gold dress uniform dated from Tudor times as did their ceremonial weapon, a long pike.

"Ruddy perfectionist," Keilty's voice came from the armchair.

Battle made a meal of his inspection.

"That's what comes of your bog regiments – no standards," reproved the Londoner.

Keilty was sprawled smoking, one arm behind his head. He laughed.

"A poet. The man's a poet. Miracles will never cease, a Londoner who can speak English," more laughter.

Battle turned away from his chore. Battle's voice was now that of a parade ground Drill Sergeant.

"Warrant Officer Gerard John Keilty, you are a disgrace to the Irish Guards. How you ever crawled out from the country to grace the Regiment with your infernal chatterings is a mystery…"

Battle broke down laughing. Keilty was wiping the tears from his eyes.

"Aye… Curbishley, to a tee… he could march forever…"

"As long as it was away from the action!" joined in Battle.

McDonald watched as his two colleagues, Henry and Fisher, both hefty bearded men, put the barrier across the gate. He stepped out of the archway.

"See you in the Social, Mac?" Henry inclined his head.

McDonald considered the notion.

"Duty first, but you might."

Henry laughed.

"I'll put one on the bar for you."

"Make mine a whisky," the voice tinged with well-worn mirth.

He watched them walk away.

"The water of life. *Slainte*," Mac sighed to himself. In the Highlands of Scotland, *Slainte* was the traditional toast given to visitors over a whisky. It was Mac's toast to life.

McDonald looked at the guardsman and nodded. The young soldier straightened his spine.

In the rounded snug of the warders' bar, Battle and Keilty were sitting with Henry. A couple of other tables were also occupied. The warders each sat with small pewter tankards in front of them. Henry cast a quizzical eye at the other two.

"How did old Doubtin' manage it? To go straight from here and become a Chelsea Pensioner."

Battle tipped back his small tankard.

"He just went in there and demanded it. Said it was his God given right as a servant of the Empire."

Keilty shook his head.

"Servant, my Great Aunt Mary. Thomas is a snob," said the lean Irishman.

It was Battle's turn to shake his head.

"But you've got to admire his gumption. He's in the Royal Hospital now, living it up in Chelsea, my son," Battle tapped the table to make his point.

"From one red coat to another," there was an ironic burr to Keilty's voice. Evan 'Doubtin'' Thomas was their friend, a former yeoman warder who, being older than them had fought as a Redcoat, serving in the British Army before its decision to issue soldiers with a more practical shade of jacket: khaki. Thomas was very proud of the fact and as a Chelsea Pensioner, he could remain in his favourite colour. He had a habit of quoting the Bible when he was in the mood, and he was always in the mood. So, being a Thomas, he had been dubbed 'Doubtin'', by Battle, in honour of the disciple, and the name had stuck.

Battle stood up, startling those around him.

"Here's to the old codger and his retirement," he announced with pomp.

Keilty and Henry exchanged a quick glance.

"Retirement, my…" said Keilty, raising his drink.

McDonald paused at the door to the Social Club. Men's deep laughter came from inside the door. He hesitated, looking back at the gate and the guardsman standing by it. He turned into the small arched door of the Social Club.

★ ★ ★

A small boat, a Thames' workhorse, with her name, *Jessie*, roughly painted over, slowly cast off from a deserted jetty. The Thames split London and the small tugs dominated the river lugging cargo up and down and across it, moving goods freshly transported in from the colonies: gold from Africa, tea from the Far East, silk from India. British goods went in the opposite direction: Manchester flannel, tools and equipment. The Thames was London's super highway.

Only now, at the darkest hour of night, was it still. Except for the lone tug.

The quayside warehouse looked run down and abandoned.

A figure, all in black, loosened the mooring rope and jumped aboard. In the distance stood the hangman's outline of Tower Bridge.

Inside the dimly lit wheelhouse, blackening was being smeared onto hands and run over faces and hair. The hair changed from blond to black. Another man pulled on a Balaclava.

A darkened pair of hands slowly sharpened a cruel curved knife, stropping it until the blade was like a razor.

* * *

The warders' snug room was now warm and busy. Keilty, Henry, Battle and Mac were still drinking at a small table. The pewter tankards now joined by stubby glasses. Battle indicated to the man behind the bar.

"Harry, four more when you're ready. No hurry."

The others laughed. Mac started to rise.

"Ought to take a turn about," Mac cocked his head towards the oak door.

Battle was having none of it.

"Give us a song, Mac. Liven the place up a bit!"

Mac looked as if he might refuse.

Henry lent his support to Battle's request.

"Go on, Mac, one from home."

A chorus of approval joined Henry's request. Mac's reluctance faded, as he stood up and moved over to stand near the bar.

Mac turned to Harry the barman and issued a challenge. "A whisky first, man!"

Grinning, Harry poured and Mac downed it to more cheers. Keilty moved to the piano in the corner. Mac stood near him. Keilty ran his fingers over the ivories.

Mac nodded to him and steadied himself. A singer's breath.

Mac's rich voice filled the warders' small, warm snug. Not only could he hold a tune, as a singer, Mac could tell a story.

The others began to join in on the chorus of *Bonnie Bonnie Scotland*. Mac's songs were the ones he had grown up with in the far north of the Scottish Highlands. He had left Scotland as a boy, to become a soldier and a man.

The others had learned his songs over time. They belted out the chorus, a choir of starkly different accents and abilities.

★ ★ ★

The small tug approached Tower Bridge. One of the painted men studied the twin towers of the bridge through small binoculars. It was a magnificent structure. Built more than 30 years ago, it remained an architectural wonder. At the time, its design was revolutionary, a combination of a bascule and suspension bridge that could allow tall vessels to pass along the Thames, by raising like a double-sided draw bridge.

★ ★ ★

Inside Tower Bridge gatehouse, Walters and Smedly, a pair of pale-faced gatekeepers, were playing cards. Enamelled tin mugs of coffee sat in front of them. Walters reached into his jacket, which was hanging on the back of his chair. He pulled out a small bottle of rum. He poured a measure into his hot drink. His companion frowned. Walters offered some to him. The other shook his head, a warning gesture.

"You'll be for it if Mason's making his rounds tonight," Smedly told Walters.

The other man shrugged and added more rum for good measure.

Two men, dressed like dockers, in long coats and caps, approached the watchman's gatehouse from the end of the bridge. Their steps hardly carried in the gloom.

★ ★ ★

The guardsman was still standing in his pillar box. He stifled a yawn and adjusted his stance.

Light spilled from the Social Club and the high-spirited Scottish singing in there.

The ravens were restless. Ruffled feathers gleamed, even in the dark.

★ ★ ★

The two men dressed as dockers stopped at the gatehouse. They checked along the bridge. One edged to the small window to look inside.

The card game was still going on. The rum was now on the table between Walters and Smedly.

The two men inched closer to the door. One continued to scan up and down the bridge. The other crouched down level with the door handle. Silently, he turned it.

A thin strangely marked pipe emerged through the small gap between the door and its frame. Walters laid down his cards.

"Rummy. You're beat," Walters gloated.

He died a winner.

A blowing sound was met by a look of surprise on Walters's face. His hand reached to his neck. A small coloured feather protruded from it. Walters was stunned, his eyes widening. Smedly looked at him and turned to the door. He started to rise as a dart stung his neck.

★ ★ ★

The bridge was opening. The boat passed beneath Tower Bridge.

★ ★ ★

The warders' club was emptying.

Mac eyed the bar as the others pulled on their jackets.

"Stay and have another," he said, glass held high.

The others shook their heads.

"Have to be up with the larks in the morn, Mac," Henry shook his head.

Mac looked across at the barman, who was clearing glasses.

"Leave the keys with me, Harry. I'll lock up," Mac's eyes were earnest.

Harry considered him for a second. He shook his head. Keilty and Battle exchanged a glance.

"Duty calls, Mac," Keilty's voice was soft.

Mac looked at his glass, sighed and nodded.

Outside, the ravens were getting edgy. Their cries echoed around the dark courtyard.

The Social Club door opened and Battle, Keilty and Henry stepped out.

"Night, Mac," Battle turned to Henry and Keilty laughing, "He's a right old soak."

Henry walked on: "Night, chaps."

Battle raised his hand in farewell.

Keilty stopped. He was listening to the ravens. He looked vaguely uneasy. Battle broke the spell.

"Mac's on the mend," said Battle believing this.

Keilty did not.

"It's only been a few months, Tommy."

Battle was defensive.

"I'm just saying."

Keilty nodded.

Battle paused, looking out over the Tower.

"Strange, Doubtin' not being here." Battle thrust his hands in his pockets.

Keilty turned back to his friend, patting him on the shoulder affectionately.

"Pious puritanical old meddler. God bless all Methodists, heathens one and all!"

Battle's good humour was restored.

Battle walked on whistling *Greensleeves*. High on the battlements a crow was watching the courtyard.

★ ★ ★

Water lapped against the side of the tug. The brooding ramparts of the Tower of London rose above it.

Chapter Two

The Raid

The guardsman stifled a yawn. He was three hours into his watch. It was going to be a long night.

Hooks, wrapped in rough cloth, came over the wall, muffling the sound as they took purchase.

Mac was standing by the ravens' cage. A slight wind tugged at his hair. Since his wife's death, sleep had been elusive. It had become his habit, checking on the ravens, before retiring to bed.

A crow took off from the battlements.

"Arck! Arck!"

The ravens in the cages became more frantic. Mac looked down from the soaring crow. Kruger grinned at him, the ridge of his scar still visible even under the black war paint.

Mac was struck from behind, sent pitching forward in the dark, his head striking the stone step.

Kruger was carrying a short spear. He stepped forward and stared at the caged birds with contempt.

"Aas (carrion)," Kruger flicked his spear towards the birds.

The ravens went wild. Kruger's smile was cruel. He turned and signalled to his men.

Shadows hugged the walls. They moved purposefully.

At the Traitor's Gate, the young guardsman lay prone, a dart in his neck.

Battle was asleep. He stirred. The ravens were screaming. He rose unsteadily.

"Not like 'em to be making a rumpus. I hope Mac's not singing to 'em again."

The shadows were working on a door. The ancient lock was resisting. The plaque beside it read 'The Jewel House'. A few feet away two guardsmen lay inert. Kruger stood poised, watching for the door to be breached.

Looking up at the White Tower, Battle swayed in the fresh air. He pulled on his coat as he moved towards the screaming birds.

Mac's pipe broke under Battle's feet. The ravens were going crazy. Battle bent down and touched Mac's tunic. Blood. Mac stirred.

From the wall a raven cried and swooped down. Battle followed its flight. Near the entrance to Traitor's Gate, figures were hauling up heavy black duffle sacs.

McDonald rose slowly.

"Blinking shoot me," breathed Battle.

"Get help, Tommy." Mac's voice was hoarse.

Battle nodded and quickly ran down the stone steps. Mac was left swaying. He spun around. Skinstad, a lean shaven-headed man, faced him with a stabbing spear. His entire skull blackened.

"You're a dead man, Engelsman," grinned Skinstad.

Skinstad jabbed the spear. Mac stumbled backwards. The blade missed him by an inch. Skinstad's teeth caught the moonlight.

On the ramparts, the shadowed men were pulling up the ropes. Sacks were being tied to ropes and hauled over the wall down to Traitor's Gate. Overseeing the operation was Otto Sturm, a huge, brawny bull-necked man. A hefty cudgel, a two-foot long rod of hard black wood, rested casually in his hand.

Battle came tearing down the stone steps and stopped short. He and Sturm froze, staring at each other.

Battle nodded slowly and raised his fists. He stepped forward. Sturm did not move. Battle threw a punch. Sturm's cudgel hit the side of Battle's head. Tommy Battle collapsed like a felled tree. Sturm prodded him with his cudgel.

Skinstad's spear snaked forward, finding its mark. Mac clutched his right arm. Mac edged back.

On the ramparts, a man began to pull up the last rope. His comrade stopped him. They could see Skinstad and Mac were facing each other, as Mac dodged backwards.

Kruger watched the combat.

"Finish him!" he hissed.

Skinstad glanced over his shoulder and nodded. Sweat poured down his face. The paint was stained.

Skinstad grinned again and struck.

McDonald stumbled, caught by the blow.

"Aaarh!"

McDonald fell away, plummeting over the wall, down an eight-foot drop. Skinstad stood clasping his spear. He hesitated.

Kruger's voice was louder, more urgent.

"Now! Come on!"

Skinstad looked down at the unconscious McDonald and made his decision. He turned and ran for the rope.

Governor Hastings looked out of the window into the courtyard, his morning ruined. *Probably, his career too.* He held a cane behind his back, a lean grey haired man with the weathered face from a lifetime of soldiering overseas.

Traditionally, the Governor of the Tower of London was

also a military man. General Hastings was cut from that cloth, serving in numerous campaigns: Sudan, India and Africa.

Battle and McDonald marched in. A pair of invalids: Battle with his head bandaged, McDonald with his arm in a sling and a gash on his cheek. Battle saluted. McDonald was unable to because of the sling and failed to hide his embarrassment.

The Governor ignored them. Even these experienced old soldiers felt uncomfortable with the silence.

When Hastings finally spoke, his voice was quiet, almost reflective.

"The ravens gone, eight guards killed and the Nation's greatest treasure vanished," the Governor's fingers ran over the cane as he talked, but his words were still directed at the window.

"The Crown Jewels have gone, stolen from under our noses. Your noses! Posing a threat to the monarchy, the sovereign power of the Empire. As if there wasn't enough unrest."

The duo stared straight ahead. The Governor turned round and fixed his eyes on them.

His tone was almost sad.

"Two of my most respected warders.

"Battle, you were with me at Ladysmith. McDonald of the Gordons."

The Governor nodded to himself, his anger rising.

His voice sharpened. Now he was facing them, icy sea eyes.

"How are your hangovers this morning, gentlemen? A bit sore, McDonald? Too blind drunk to see where you were going? Walking into someone's blade?"

"No, sir." McDonald stared straight over the Governor's head.

Hastings sucked in his breath. He leaned in slightly.

"When I want an answer I'll ask for one."

"Yes, sir." McDonald grimaced at his mistake. Battle

swallowed nervously. The Governor struggled to collect himself.

The space between Hastings and the objects of his wrath closed to a matter of inches.

"At this moment in time, your records mean nothing. Nothing."

The Governor sat down to gather himself.

"When Thomas left I considered you for promotion, McDonald," Hastings spoke almost to himself.

He looked up. The sea-green of his glance had darkened. A storm gathering.

"The Prime Minister is furious, the War Office is looking for scapegoats and the king...

"Can you remember anything, McDonald?"

McDonald hesitated.

"It's all a bit hazy, sir," McDonald admitted.

Hastings snapped his cane on the desk.

"I'll bet it is. Perhaps I can aid your failing memory. Two watchmen on the Bridge were found dead. Not a mark on them. Likewise, six of the guards. The other two were strangled. Two of the ravens have returned so far.

"Not a bad night's work, wouldn't you say?"

There was no answer this time from the yeomen warders. Hastings was on his feet again, retreating to his window.

"And all we've been left with is two hungover yeoman warders and a polite little note."

The Governor picked up a piece of paper from his desk, a shadow of cold amusement on his face.

"Thank'ee kindly for your loan, Ma'Lord King. Signed Colonel Blood."

The warders' expressions tightened. The thief was mocking them and the Crown.

Hastings appeared to have come to a decision.

"The Tower has been closed to the public until further notice. Dangerous masonry, the kind of work that may take months to finish. You two are confined to quarters, pending a full inquiry. Dismissed!"

Two guardsmen escorted Mac and Battle across the Tower courtyard. The young soldiers glanced at their charges with a mix of hostility and embarrassment. Keilty watched from a doorway. As they marched past the White Tower, Keilty nodded to the Guardsmen and at Battle and McDonald. Battle pursed his lips. McDonald stared straight ahead.

Battle's living room was crowded with the three warders within it. Keilty lit a cigarette. Battle sat with his head in his hands.

"Christ, anyone'd think we'd stolen the ruddy Crown Jewels ourselves," Battle looked at the others for support.

McDonald did not spare him.

"We did. Just as surely as if we had lifted them ourselves, Tommy."

Battle shook his head, his eyes on Mac.

"Who could have done it? The damn treacherous Irish!"

Keilty reacted in a flash.

"Hold your tongue!"

Battle and Keilty squared up. Battle the bulkier, but Keilty's stance was that of a fighter, too.

Battle snarled into his friend's face; an outlet for his frustration.

"All they're fit for is rebellion and mutiny."

Keilty was ready to explode. Battle was itching to light the fuse.

McDonald placed his hands gently on their shoulders. He was bigger than both and somehow calm despite the tension.

"Stop it, you idiots. Step down. It wasn't the Irish."

Battle and Keilty had their eyes fixed on each other.

McDonald sighed.

"It wasn't the Irish."

Battle cast a sideways glance at Mac. Keilty was still staring at Battle.

McDonald leaned in.

"Where do you stand, Ged?"

Keilty looked from Battle to Mac. His eyes on them, he nodded slowly. McDonald stepped away, giving the other men space.

"The one who stabbed me. He spoke to me."

Battle's face was incredulous.

"You told the General you couldn't remember," he pointed a finger at Mac.

McDonald shrugged.

"Since when have you told an officer all you know? The thief spoke. He called me an Engelsman."

The other two stared at him.

McDonald was definite.

"He was South African."

Battle sat down.

"The Boers. The filthy…"

Keilty cut in.

"Shut up, Tommy."

Keilty looked at McDonald.

"What's on your mind, Mac?"

McDonald flexed his fingers.

"First, I want to speak to Thomas."

Battle looked confused.

"Doubtin'? But he's in Chelsea."

"And we're all confined to barracks," pointed out Keilty.

McDonald tugged off his sling, with a slight wince.

He stood up.

"Then we go AWOL."

The others stared at him. To go Absent Without Leave

21

meant abandoning all that they stood for: their duty, their careers as soldiers and yeoman warders. They would become outlaws.

Chapter Three

Flight of the Ravens

A large cargo vessel, the *Isaac Hamilton*, was berthed at the quayside of the Victoria Docks. It was taking on cargo for the West Coast of Africa. Two police officers walked up the gangplank and they were met by a nervous seaman. One of the constables was offered a document for inspection. Further along the quayside, other boats were being boarded. The operation to track down the stolen jewels was underway.

★ ★ ★

In his quarters, Battle was taking off his uniform. He did it with great care and thought, picking a speck off the jacket; a solemn farewell.

★ ★ ★

A police van pulled up in front of the entrance to King's Cross railway station. The Bobbies fanned out, moving through the crowd, while the police sergeant made his way to the station master's office.

The station master, a small bespectacled man, read a letter dangled in front of him by Sergeant Hollins. Two other police officers waited.

The station master looked up, a question on his face.

"May I ask what we are looking for?"

The policemen looked at each other.

The senior man, Sergeant Hollins, gave the answer.

"Anything suspicious, in particular, any large cargoes. But nothing must be done to attract the attention of the public."

★ ★ ★

Keilty stood in front of a mirror in his bedroom. He was now in civvies. He pulled on a cap.

"Straight out of the bog, Ged," Keilty doffed his cap to himself.

★ ★ ★

The room was dark and opulent, a club for gentlemen, of the kind reserved for the influential, the powerful and the wealthy.

The Empire had given rise to many such establishments. This one had been founded in 1810, just before Wellington's victory at Waterloo.

Two distinguished men, Viscount Crombie and Sir Charles Everett, sipped drinks in plush leather chairs. Both were affluent gentlemen in dark suits.

Crombie was the elder man. He measured his words, like pouring a drink.

"Britain will be a laughing stock. It will undermine the king and the Government's standing abroad. We do not want another Russia here."

Sir Charles nodded.

A shiver went through both men. Just six years earlier, Lenin's Bolsheviks had stormed the Winter Palace in a bloody revolution. In the aftermath, the Tsar of Russia and his family had been murdered and a new power had arisen. Communism was spreading. The fear was that Germany would be the next State to fall prey to it. The terror was that such an uprising might happen on British shores. Sir Charles took a sip of his drink to help wash away that thought.

"Agreed. What's to be done?"

Viscount Crombie counted out his response.

"All boats on the Thames are being searched. Stations are being watched. It's vital that we do not cause widespread alarm. The Prime Minister is furious. Heads will roll for this," Crombie raised a finger towards a steward.

Sir Charles leaned forward.

"Any clues to who might have been behind all this?"

Crombie's irritation showed.

"Absolutely none. Except a short, impudent note from Colonel Blood," Crombie's face coloured as he used the word.

Sir Charles sat back, a slow nod.

"Our thief knows his history, then."

The Viscount was flushed now; a cocktail of anger and port.

"Charles II may have pardoned that Blood, but it's doubtful this one will escape without spilling his. About time," he said, as a waiter arrived with a note on a tray.

In a nearby seat, a gentleman was sitting in a deep recess, wrapped in shadow. He was still, as a snake before it strikes. In his hand, he was slowly turning a black cane with a worn handle, its top carved in the shape of a wolf's head.

★ ★ ★

A row of medals was laid on top of a citation. The aged writing on it carried the briefest details of an afternoon of carnage and death in the mountains of Northern India. It had been a deadly mission. McDonald had gone native, working his way among the mountain paths, wrapped against the dry wind, his rifle bound in rags to keep the dust out. It was there he had cemented his reputation. Dirty work, ending in a bloody gunfight.

McDonald picked them up: silk, metal, paper and ink. The colour of a couple of the ribbons had faded. The early additions of his collection. He looked around his room.

His gaze was slow.

"Thirty years," his voice was hardly more than a murmur.

McDonald straightened. He was in civilian clothes now. He put the medals in a small wooden box. Next to them he placed a portrait picture of a young couple. His fingers brushed the woman's face in the picture. She smiled back just as she had when they first met. Her smile had never wavered; from their wedding day to when she had died in this small room. It was the one wound he still carried.

"Wish me luck, Eileen."

Eileen had followed the drum, she had been a dutiful soldier's wife, seen the world and disliked most of it. The heat, the dirt, the worry that her husband would be ambushed and left in a shallow grave. Only when Mac had become a warder at the Tower had she found a measure of contentment. It had given her a sense of home and place. Then illness had crept up on her. She had been frail even before that. She had supported him, needed him, yet resented the soldier in him. In going AWOL, Mac realised he was leaving behind more than the Tower and his life as a warder, he was also bidding Eileen farewell.

He wrapped the picture and the medals in a strip of rough khaki cloth and closed the drawer. He would be travelling light on this mission.

The Tower gates were open. Two guardsmen stood under the archway. A military policeman was talking to them.

A small crowd was at the gates, where Yeoman Warder Henry was flanked by a couple of police constables.

Henry was beginning to look a mite exasperated. There

was a repetitive note to his voice.

"All I know, madam, is that the falling masonry is dangerous," as he turned to face the next questioner.

A figure stepped into the courtyard. He was carrying a ladder on his shoulder and a small, flat wooden box case in his other hand. His boots made a heavy grating noise on the stone.

At an angle, high above him, Governor Hastings was standing at his window. He watched the figure, a small frown growing as realisation dawned.

Hastings turned in panic from his vantage point, calling out for his deputy: "Moss!"

The workman reached the gate. He tugged his cap down.

The military police officer on duty turned towards him.

Keilty touched his cap.

"It's gonna take weeks to fix that stonework, guv."

The military policeman nodded. Keilty steered away from the back of the yeoman warder. The disguised yeoman was smiling broadly.

Along a narrow lane beneath the Tower's shadow, a manhole opened. Tommy Battle hauled himself and a small bundle out of the hole. He looked up and down the quiet street, replaced the sewer lid and walked away, whistling. *Greensleeves* echoed along the lane. The Tower of London rose behind him.

A small arched door opened as the Governor ran out in to the courtyard with two yeoman warders following. They headed towards the gate, part run, part panic.

In a narrow alley, known as Mint Street, a small cart was being loaded with the Tower laundry.

The task of carrying the large sacks of laundry fell to the young auxiliaries. It was a two-man job, moving the sacks from a small washroom, through a narrow arched alley into Mint Street, where the cart was tethered. The older of the two men, Rob, offered his colleague a smoke. John hesitated, took a quick draw, then lifted another handful of sacks, before turning out along the dark passage. John stepped out into the sunlight.

The auxiliary stopped in his tracks. Behind him, Rob's cigarette fell from his mouth. The cart had gone.

* * *

In the stained glass lit gloom of the chapel at the Royal Hospital Chelsea, Evan Thomas was setting out hymnbooks. He was older than his former colleagues at the Tower. Dressed in the red tunic of a Chelsea Pensioner, Thomas's angled face was topped by close-cropped iron-grey, almost spiky, hair. A serious looking man, he was humming to himself. He made one last check that everything was in order and left.

Thomas, resplendent in his red tunic, stood adjusting to the sunlight, with his hands tucked behind his back, and gazed at the wide red-bricked palisade.

The Royal Hospital Chelsea had been built in 1692 on the orders of King Charles II and designed by his favourite architect, Sir Christopher Wren. It provided a home for retired soldiers and Thomas felt very much at home here.

Thomas turned left. He walked slowly through the archway.

He strolled past a gardener working on a small area of soil in front of an open window. As Thomas passed, the gardener started whistling. The tune was *Greensleeves*.

Thomas frowned and moved his head slightly, glancing back at the kneeling figure.

The gardener looked up.

"Looking well, Doubtin'. Retirement suits you," Battle

sat back on his haunches and grinned up at the astonished Thomas.

"What the devil!"

Battle shook his head in reproach.

"Tut, tut. No blasphemy please. Doesn't suit you."

Battle's grin widened, as Thomas reined in his amazement.

Thomas sat back in a comfy chair. Keilty relaxed on the simple bed. Battle was perched at the foot of the bed, shoulders hunched. McDonald was pacing, restless. Not that there was much, if any, room to pace. Thomas's room was a wooden panelled cupboard, with dark shutters aside the windows. Mac had to turn with every second stride.

Thomas lit his pipe, his eyes on Mac's broad frame.

"You're certain that's what he actually said, Mac?"

McDonald stopped mid-prowl.

"Yes. Yes, I am. Damn certain."

Thomas raised an eyebrow at the language. Mac turned to face him.

"It wasn't just the Afrikaans. The spear," McDonald touched his wounded arm, "it was a Zulu stabbing spear."

Battle was confused. "What, they was Zulus?"

Keilty studied McDonald's face.

McDonald took his time.

"No, they had blackening on. He was sweating. It began to run off," he said more quietly.

Thomas seemed far away, gathering his response. The others waited.

"Um, hum. Why didn't you tell the Governor, Mac?"

Thomas turned to the others: "Why go AWOL?"

The word hung for a beat between them. Its repercussions magnified in Thomas's cramped quarters.

Keilty met the Welshman's steady gaze.

"We messed up. It was our charge and we failed. Mac

didn't tell Hastings and I wouldn't have either. This is our fight," he said.

Battle's face was earnest, but there was a hint of unease.

"You too, Thomas. You gonn'a turn us in?"

Thomas smoked his pipe. He smiled wryly.

"Here we are. The Four Ravens."

Thomas stood up. His decision made.

"The theft was carried out by Boers, a group of at least 30 or so. They approached by boat, scaled the south wall. Disabled the guards."

"Killed 'em. And the ravens?" Battle cut in.

Thomas was still thinking aloud.

"The first place to look would be the docks," he paused only to raise an eyebrow at Battle.

"Right," agreed the stocky Londoner.

Thomas took another draw on his pipe.

"That's where the authorities will look, too."

"There won't be any way out via the Thames. But we may find something down there. I suggest…"

"I'm going to see Laird," McDonald's words stilled the company.

The others looked at him.

Thomas nodded slowly.

"Your old CO. Are you sure he won't just turn you in?"

McDonald shook his head.

"I saved his life, he saved mine."

Thomas's next words were dry.

"And he got the tin." Another smoke ring billowed out. Keilty and Battle watched the exchange. McDonald dug his heels in.

"He was with intelligence in Natal. He'll help," McDonald was adamant.

Thomas nodded slowly, but looked vaguely uneasy.

"We'll do the docks. My old stomping ground," Battle

cocked his head towards Keilty, who gave the barest of nods.

Thomas took another puff of his pipe.

"You and Ged cover the docklands. They must have hired or bought the boat. Find it. Find that and you'll find their base. But be careful and another thing – trim your whiskers. You too, Mac," Thomas pointed his pipe at Battle then McDonald.

Battle touched his sideburns lovingly. Keilty nodded. Mac looked defiant, but Thomas had not finished.

"You go and speak to Lord Laird. If nothing else, he's an expert in South African affairs," Thomas's expression was at odds with his words.

Thomas picked up a folded paper.

"Always writing in *The Times*, he is."

Battle pulled on his jacket.

"What about you, Doubtin'? Railway stations?"

Thomas considered the question.

"No, I rather fancy a trip to the British Library," he said absently.

The others looked puzzled as he relit his pipe. Keilty managed a wry smile. He'd known Evan 'Doubtin'' Thomas a long time.

Chapter Four

The Hunt Begins

Wapping High Street was a narrow vein of commerce. Cobbled in parts, it was lined with tall warehouses, crammed with goods shipped in from all corners of the globe.

Battle and Keilty walked with purpose along the busy East End street. Their majestic red embroidered uniforms were gone. Instead, they matched their surroundings. Two dock workers in course jackets and tough working hob-nail boots.

Ahead of them, they spied two police constables walking in their direction. Battle checked.

"Peelers straight ahead," he breathed out of the side of his mouth.

Keilty stopped him from turning around.

"How are they going to recognise you? You with no whiskers on, Tommy."

Battle ran his hand over his clean shaven jaw as they kept walking.

"Blinking shoot me. I'd clean forgot," Battle started to chuckle.

They passed the two policemen through the crowd, stepping aside as a large crate was lowered from one of the high warehouse windows.

"Where's our first port of call?" The Irishman's question was a whisper.

Battle now led the way. This was his territory.

"The *Star and Garter*, my son. See if our Jack's still in

business," Battle strode forward. Keilty nodded, his pace more measured.

★ ★ ★

McDonald came out from the crowd of the underground station. He blinked to allow his eyes to adjust to the sunlight. He seldom used the underground railway, being closed in reminded him too much of the tunnels and trenches of Flanders. He paused at the memory: sitting in the mud and darkness waiting for a hint of movement across the barren No Man's Land. Waiting to shoot the helmet off some careless German.

Mac had also discarded his uniform, but he still had his whiskers. He paused to get his bearings. Behind him a newspaper seller was plying his trade.

"Bloody Tower closure latest!"

McDonald frowned, decided on a direction and walked.

★ ★ ★

The bar in the *Star and Garter* was busy, and raucous with rough laughter. Keilty was sitting in an alcove, nursing a tankard. As was his custom, he had half an eye on the door. Keilty had learned early always to have an exit plan. It had kept him alive this long.

Battle edged his way towards Keilty through the crowded bar.

"Excuse me, guv. Ta," he said, as he worked his way back through the crammed pub.

Battle leaned with his arms on the back of an empty chair, facing his friend. Keilty raised a quizzical eyebrow. Battle shook his head.

"No joy. Jack's running a boozer in Bermondsey."

Keilty nodded and finished his pint. They were heading south of the river. Battle had other ideas.

"Here, hold on, asking questions is thirsty work."

Battle turned back towards the bar. Keilty moved to protest, but he was too late.

Battle stepped up to the bar and the barmaid offered him a tired smile.

"Yes, dear?"

A well-built man in his twenties, a docker from his garb, moved to block Battle out.

"Two pints and two gins," ordered the dockworker.

Battle's frown was small.

"Excuse me, guv."

The docker turned slowly. His look was dismissive and quietly threatening.

"Yes, old timer?"

The docker's mates began to take an interest. Confident amused smiles. They had seen this sideshow before. It was part of their regular entertainment.

Behind Battle, Keilty was rising from his seat. The barmaid looked from the hefty docker to the older and much shorter Battle.

Battle cocked his head on one side and smiled up at the larger younger man.

"You ever heard of the expression 'Age before beauty'? I thought not, 'cos you're an ugly mug."

The docker's grin evaporated. He lunged for Battle.

The old soldier planted his first punch directly on the docker's nose and his second on his jaw. The docker dropped to the floorboards coughing up blood.

Battle's fists were still up. He stared around the bar.

"What about 'Looks can be deceiving'? Ever heard that one?" Battle asked, standing over the injured man.

Even this tough bar was stunned. Keilty reached his friend.

Keilty hissed at Battle.

"What are you trying to do?"

Battle resisted Keilty's pull just long enough to take a swig of the docker's pint from the bar and grace the barmaid with a wink.

★ ★ ★

Sir Charles Everett's office overlooked Horseguards' Parade. A wide sanded expanse used primarily by the Guards' Regiments for their drill exercises and as the venue for the annual Trooping the Colour ceremony.

The room was splendid, blessed with tall windows and a high ceiling, dominated by a huge desk. A headmaster's study without the books.

Governor Hastings had made the hurried journey here from the Tower. He sat facing Sir Charles across the wide grand wooden desk.

Outside, guards were rehearsing for Trooping the Colour. The dull crunch of their boots provided the soundtrack to the discussion.

Sir Charles held up a file. It read 'THOMAS ALBERT BATTLE'. Beneath it were two further files.

Sir Charles Everett read from the file in crisp tones.

"Battle, Thomas Albert, Warrant Officer Class I. Royal London Fusiliers. Combined Services Middleweight boxing champion 1897."

Governor Hastings nodded. He looked uncomfortable to be answering questions, cast in the role of an errant schoolboy due to the actions of his men.

"At three different weights. Later coached the army team. Olympic Gold London, 1908."

Sir Charles studied the interruption, before looking at another file.

He read another excerpt.

"Keilty, Gerard Patrick John. WOI Irish Guards. My God. The Somme Sniper. More than 1,000 kills."

"McDonald was reputed to have been even better," said Hastings.

Sir Charles's exasperation showed.

"These are unblemished records, exemplary. What could possibly have turned these men into traitors?"

"Perhaps they are not, Sir."

The civil servant regarded the Governor. Hastings met his gaze.

"Perhaps they are gone to track down the thieves," Hastings suggestion was a quiet one, almost hopeful.

Sir Charles was dismissive.

"I understand your loyalty, General, but these men are involved up to their eyeballs," Sir Charles tapped one of the files, "this McDonald chap. I think he's the ringleader."

The Governor frowned slightly.

"Well, he hasn't been the same since his wife died last year, but I'm …"

This time, the interruption came from Sir Charles.

"We'll find them and when we do, we'll find the jewels."

The files dropped from his hand with a flat thud onto his desk.

★ ★ ★

McDonald stopped to check his appearance in the window of a small corner shop then turned to cross the street. He touched his fine whiskers. He did so to avoid a portly police constable sauntering towards him. This was a respected, refined part of London. Unlike Wapping, policemen did not have to patrol in pairs here.

★ ★ ★

Keilty and Battle hurried along a gloomy, dank alley. They passed a sign: 'Hangman's Lane'. Keilty checked and studied the sign, nodding slightly with grim humour. However, the Irishman did not stop, Keilty was pushing the pace.

Despite his low voice, Keilty was furious.

"You jackass. What was that all about? Just because you wanted a pint."

Battle tried to stop to explain.

"Ged. Sorry, Ged. It's just the worry. The jewels, and everything."

Keilty kept him moving.

"Worry, my great aunt. We're going to find Jack and you can save your combinations for when we find us them Boers," Keilty's voice was edged.

★ ★ ★

Less than a mile away, Neils Skinstad, a tall man with startling cold blue eyes and a shaven head, was standing in an arched double doorway of a warehouse. He looked relaxed yet watchful. He threw away a cigarette and scanned along the street from his vantage point. He was acting as lookout.

Inside the warehouse, men were working. They were carefully packing crates. The large crates had stamps on them: 'Fragile Antiques'. Van Sturm was overseeing the men, while Kruger was walking along inspecting the seals on the crates.

The small hatch door in the arched wooden double doors opened. Kruger swung around. All the men tensed. Skinstad grinned at them from the doorway. Kruger looked annoyed. He and Van Sturm exchanged a glance. The men breathed a collective sigh of relief and started working again.

★ ★ ★

Keilty was standing outside the *Tea Clipper*. Casual and watchful like a man waiting for a friend to join him. A couple passed him to walk into the public house as Battle hurried out.

"The *Three Bells*, Rotherhithe."

The pair moved on quickly.

Inside the long narrow bar, a ferret of a barman was polishing glasses at the end nearest the door. The *Lucky Sailor*, formerly the *Three Bells* was a narrow, poorly lit bar. Three men were standing at the bar, cupping their drinks. A small card school occupied one corner. Gin rummy was the game of choice. Battle and Keilty pushed the small double door open. All the men noted their arrival. The *Lucky Sailor* always offered that kind of welcome to strangers, cold and silent.

★ ★ ★

McDonald climbed the steps to the door of an imposing townhouse. He studied the small plaque by the polished wooden door. 'Lord Laird DSO'. Without thinking, Mac's hand went to his tie.

A manservant, Campbell, led McDonald along a tiled hallway. MacDonald studied the manservant. Campbell was an imposing, powerfully built sikh. Campbell's boots were military issue.

The sikh was a huge man, one of the legendary fighting Frontier Force. Mac recalled that the man he had come to see, Lord Laird, had commanded the sikhs in Afghanistan and later China. MacDonald had met Campbell before. He might polish the silverware these days, but Mac sensed

Campbell would be adept with the other uses for a knife.

The pair entered a tastefully decorated living room.

Campbell stood to attention.

"Regimental Sergeant Major McDonald, M'Lord."

Lord Magnus Laird was seated at an antique desk. He was a tall, distinguished man, with a bearing accustomed to command. He looked quizzically as McDonald entered. McDonald stopped in the middle of the room.

Laird acknowledged his visitor.

"McDonald."

"Sir."

Laird and Campbell exchanged a glance. Laird gave a subtle hand signal that was not lost on McDonald. Laird rose, as Campbell withdrew.

Laird stopped at a small table.

"A dram, McDonald." It was an order.

He poured without waiting for a reply.

"*Slainte.*"

"*Slainte.*"

★ ★ ★

Small lights illuminated the secluded reading corners inside the library at the British Museum. Thomas was sitting at a shadowed table. He was still in his red Chelsea Pensioner's coat. He should have changed out of it before journeying to the library, but his mission was urgent.

A librarian carried over another volume of papers.

Thomas nodded his thanks as he turned a page. The headline read "Victory at Ladysmith from Our Correspondent with Roberts' Army".

The siege had lasted more than 100 days. Battle had fought in the dugouts and the gun pits, without clean water and scant food. Thomas gently rubbed his nose. It wasn't

Battle's kind of fight, but he had survived it. He remembered Battle saying casually, one summer evening as they strolled the Tower courtyard, that to be wounded at Ladysmith was to die. By the time General Buller's relief force had punched a way through Botha's surrounding Boer troops, Battle's twenty-strong platoon had been reduced to two desperate starving men. The relief of Ladysmith had been celebrated as a great victory. Thomas adjusted his spectacles and read on.

★ ★ ★

Battle and Keilty were sitting nursing a drink, watching. The *Lucky Sailor* was filling up. Men determined to wash away the day's toil.

"Ask the barman," Keilty's voice was low.

Battle took a sip of his drink.

"Patience, my son." Battle sat back to wait. He was in his element.

★ ★ ★

Laird and McDonald were sitting opposite each other. Their expressions quiet and intense.

Laird studied the warder, sitting uncomfortably in his civvies. McDonald had never felt comfortable out of uniform. For his part, Laird was immaculately turned out, Savile Row and Jermyn Street tailors, London's finest attire.

"You're sure, then? He was a Boer."

McDonald sat forward and nodded.

Laird's gaze was direct.

"But you were drunk," he said, raising his hand to forestall McDonald's objection.

"We all like a dram, man. I'm not saying you were spliced," Laird's tone was reasonable, unhurried. "But consider, you had indulged, he had struck you. Might you not be mistaken?"

McDonald shook his head.

"No, sir. He spoke to me first. Before anything else happened, just after I had found the ravens were gone," McDonald paused, then decided to go on.

"He was a Boer."

Laird considered him.

Laird's next question was almost indifferent.

"Would you recognise him?" he asked.

McDonald did not need to answer.

Laird flexed his fingers.

"I see. Why didn't you inform Governor Hastings of your suspicions?"

McDonald nursed his whisky. "I dinna ken." He looked up. "It's my responsibility. My duty."

Laird studied him a moment. He sighed slightly.

Laird nodded.

"Mine, too. What next, McDonald? What's your strategy?"

McDonald's next breath was relief.

"That's where we thought you might help," his face was earnest.

Laird measured the man before him, for a moment his thoughts were on another day, 25 years earlier, in the Veldt.

"I'll do all I can. But I need to know which avenues you've exhausted already."

McDonald saw the sense in this.

"Ged and Tommy are scouring the docks. It's Tommy's manor. He still has family down there," McDonald explained.

Laird nodded. He took a small, thoughtful sip of his drink.

Chapter Five

Rooftop Escape

The *Lucky Sailor* was getting busier. Battle and Keilty were sitting in the same seats. Keilty got up and moved to the bar.

He signalled the barman.

"Two more, if you please," Keilty placed a coin on the worn polished surface.

Men at the bar eyed the Irishman. His accent had marked him. He smiled benevolently at them.

Keilty looked down towards the end of the bar. A man was sitting on a chair beside a small door. Keilty looked at the mirrored wall of the bar and moved his head.

Battle, watching Keilty's reflection, followed the movement of Keilty's head. Battle nodded very slowly.

Keilty turned with the pints. Battle followed him as they walked down the bar. The barman noticed their direction, put down a glass and moved parallel with them. The young man sitting on the chair sensed their approach and started to rise.

Keilty's voice became a thick Irish brogue.

"Top of the morning to you."

The man was standing. Keilty threw the contents of one of the pints into the man's face. Battle turned the handle of the small door and strode inside.

Battle barged in. The three men were gathered around a low table, their faces registering shock.

Dave, sparse and mean, reacted first. "What?"

Dave pulled out a cosh. He liked a fight.

Battle ignored him, stepping forward.

Jack was scrambling to brush some small jewellery pieces into a black velvet bag. Jack was a stocky man in his early twenties. Dave, thin and agressive, kept moving with the cosh.

Keilty threw the contents of his second pint into Dave's face and jabbed him in the guts, deftly removing the cosh as the younger man collapsed.

Battle stayed poised on his toes.

"Evening, Jack."

Jack stared at Battle. He looked at the wounded Dave, as Alan, a callow teenager, pulled out a knife and faced Battle and Keilty.

Battle grinned at Jack. He flicked his gaze to Alan.

"Put it away, son," Battle's eyes were back on Jack. "Long time no see, Jack."

Jack held up the small black bag.

"Just small beer compared to you, Uncle Tommy."

Battle accepted the compliment.

"We need to talk, privy like."

The barman at the door and Alan looked at Jack for guidance.

Jack pointed at his minders.

"Get out!"

He pointed at Dave, still struggling to sit up on the floor.

"And take him with you." Jack turned to his Uncle Tommy Battle and grinned.

★ ★ ★

Thomas sat back and took off his small spectacles to rub the bridge of his nose. To an observer, it might have appeared to indicate a certain weariness. In fact, it was a mannerism that showed Thomas had come to a decision.

The only sounds in the library were the slow breaths of concentration and the turning of pages.

On a piece of paper next to him, Thomas had written in

pencil: 'Ladysmith', 'Reitfontein' and 'Johannesburg Commando'. He glanced about him.

"God forgive this poor sinner," whispered Thomas.

Carefully he took out a small knife and cut along the newspaper, coughing to cover the sound.

He studied the article again and nodded in a tight determined fashion.

★ ★ ★

Laird and McDonald were at the front door, as McDonald prepared to take his leave. Laird was giving instructions. He was back in command.

"Remember, you've gone AWOL. Trust no one. The three of you must act quickly, but with caution. I'll get word to you at the *Bull and Bush*, and McDonald, thank you for coming to me. I'll get word to you tomorrow."

McDonald nodded. Laird extended his hand. McDonald shook it with pride.

"Thank you, sir," said McDonald.

Laird's grip tightened. "*Bydand.*"

The regimental motto of the Gordon Highlanders: Steadfast and Endure.

McDonald held the grip and the gaze.

"*Bydand.*" They would face this together.

Laird rang a small bell. Campbell appeared with another manservant, Argyle, a narrow mean-faced sikh, slighter than his compatriot and younger.

Laird nodded to McDonald, as he left.

Laird was peering through the lace netting, watching as McDonald crossed the road. His lordship looked thoughtful. Campbell was waiting by the door.

"I'm going to my Club, Campbell."

Campbell gave the barest of nods.

"Do you remember McDonald?"

Campbell's nod was slow, given with almost an exaggerated care.

"Yes, sir, of the Gordons, sir."

"His father was one of our ghillies at Glengoyne, later head gamekeeper. Damn fine shot. Always shot to kill."

Campbell passed Lord Laird his hat, gloves and cane.

★ ★ ★

Thomas had laid out his findings on his bed. Although his room at the Royal Hospital was small and cramped, Thomas found it comfortable. As a soldier, yeoman warder or in his present position, Thomas's needs had always been simple and Spartan.

Thomas laid his pipe on the arm of his straight-backed wooden chair and started to unbutton his red jacket. Thomas paused to pick up a piece of paper. He studied it for a couple of seconds. Satisfied, he eased off his tunic.

★ ★ ★

Battle, Keilty and Jack were sitting at a small table, drinks in front of them.

Battle was exasperated.

"You don't know of any others, Jack? Either side of the river."

Jack pursed his lips.

"Na, nothing. I'll put out the word, Tommy."

Battle stood. Keilty followed.

"The *Bull and Bush*, Jack," said Battle.

Jack nodded.

The door to Jack's den opened. The barman stood aside for Battle and Keilty as they stepped out. The barman cast them a strange look and closed the door. Dave, sitting holding his head, gave the pair a more hostile look. As Battle and Keilty walked away, the Irishman turned to Battle.

"Think he'll find anything?"

Battle paused for a second.

"This is his manor. If there's a sniff, he'll find it."

Keilty nodded, almost to himself, as they stepped into the London gloom.

"If they're in his manor."

★ ★ ★

Thomas, now in a tweed suit, pulled on a dark coat. He drew aside his jacket, revealing the smooth curved handle of a weapon. Thomas tugged on a cap and reached to turn off the light. He, too, was going AWOL.

★ ★ ★

Poised, in the black recess of a warehouse doorway, Skinstad edged closer to the wall. Across the street, two police constables were on patrol, clapping their hands to ward off the chill. Skinstad watched them. He'd heard them before he'd spied them. The policemen stopped in front of the warehouse, where Kruger and his men were working. The officers were holding a muted discussion. They moved apart as though circling the warehouse.

"Night, Fred!" The other officer raised his hand in farewell.

Skinstad was too far away to hear the words. He slipped a blade into his hand.

★ ★ ★

The *Bull and Bush* was a building of faded pomp and scant

glory. A tall, three-story public house that stood on the corner where, strangely, three streets met. The curved façade added to its air of welcome, although both its door and windows looked bleached, weathered and uncared for. It was a pub now past its prime.

All three streets that led to it were still. Yet the vicinity was not deserted.

A police van was emptying of officers. Two military policemen were with them.

A black car pulled up. Two senior police officers and a man in smart civilian dress began to climb out. The Commissioner of Police, a stout red-faced man, Inspector Reeves, slimmer and fitter looking than his commanding officer and Sir Charles Everett, who looked agitated.

"How good is your information, Commissioner?"

The Commissioner signalled to his subordinate and Reeves took his cue.

"It was an anonymous call, sir. Simply said that the three warders, who had disappeared from the Tower, were in the *Bull and Bush*.

"There are only two such named premises in the city, sir. The other one is being raided…" Reeves glanced at his watch. "… just about now, sir."

Sir Charles grunted.

"Very good. Carry on, Inspector."

The police officer began to turn away, but Sir Charles had not finished.

"Inspector, there's to be no mess. We need to know why these men went AWOL. There could be a lot more at stake if we don't," Sir Charles watched Reeves walk towards the corner pub. "They must know something."

In a small dingy room in the *Bull and Bush*, McDonald was asleep. His eyes opened. Instantly alert, he could feel the warning prang between his shoulder blades.

Police Sergeant Larry Tucker, a blunt-faced bruiser, waved a squad of constables into place. They were carrying sledgehammers. Across the road, soldiers had taken up position, their rifles trained on the upstairs windows.

The sergeant held up his hand, waiting. He looked across the street. Inspector Reeves nodded to him. The sergeant dropped his hand.

The pub's door caved in.

Police constables kicked their way in, trying to avoid the jagged splinters as the door gave way under the assault. The sergeant directed them either side of the bar and pointed upstairs. The officers rushed to obey.

A thin wire, invisible to all but careful eyes, was stretched across the top of the first flight of stairs, about six inches from the floorboards. The police charged up the stairs. A large polished boot caught the wire. The leading officer went down heavily, the crack of a bone breaking his fall.

There was a pile up on the stairs.

Sergeant Tucker was furious.

"What the flamin' hell…? Move it!" he hissed.

The police scrambled up the stairs.

The door to McDonald's room crashed open. Two officers charged in. One checked the wardrobe, the other beneath the bed with his boot.

"Nothing here, sarge," reported the first Constable.

Sergeant Tucker urged them on.

"Upstairs. Move it!"

Police officers dashed along the hallway. Two shoulders together, they barged into another room. Along the corridor, two more officers had got hold of a seedy-looking man in his nightclothes.

Tucker shook his head. This was plainly not who they had come for.

"Take him downstairs."

The man was struggling.

"What the devil…? This is my pub," said the enraged landlord.

Tucker leaned in close to the man.

"Shut up. You're for the high jump." Tucker was already turning away.

"What…?" The landlord was confused, a bruising mixture of shock, interrupted sleep and the fear of the truncheon in his ribs.

A dazed woman was dragged out of a door by more officers. A half-dressed man was pulled out of the same room. Both were protesting.

Tucker turned back to the innkeeper.

"We'll start with harbouring known criminals," Tucker's smile had no mirth in it.

The sergeant cast an eye at the woman as she was manhandled down the stairs. She glowered at him.

"But perhaps we'll have to look in to other illegal activities. Get this squealing pig out of here." Tucker pointed at the distressed woman and turned away. He had other quarry.

Tucker continued his journey upstairs.

Two officers reached the top floor. Both were short of breath. A small attic style door was slightly ajar. The officers looked at each other, tightened the grips on their truncheons and nodded to each other. Gathering courage.

The leading officer pushed the door open and walked in, onto a fist.

Battle skipped out as if in the boxing ring. Behind him, Keilty was climbing out of a skylight. Mac's face appeared above the skylight.

"What in heaven's name is he doing?" Mac asked Keilty.

Keilty looked back through the door. Battle delivered a

second blow to the first policeman's midriff. He went down. Battle faced his colleague.

The constable readied himself.

"Right, no more of that malarkey." But he sounded already beaten.

He looked at Battle. The old soldier altered his stance and edged forward.

Keilty swung down from the skylight.

"Tommy. For heaven's sake."

The policeman looked uncertain. He glanced behind Battle, who had his guard up.

"Sarge! Up..."

Battle caught him with a straight jab. The policeman's head snapped back. As he tried to regain his balance, Battle followed the combination through and the officer fell back crashing through the banister.

"Tommy!" Keilty grabbed hold of Battle.

Battle looked down as the officer landed on his colleagues crammed below. He gave a satisfied smile. He wasn't losing his touch.

Sergeant Tucker looked down at the sprawled mass of limbs and uniforms, where the falling officer landed.

Tucker stared at the twisted carnage at his feet.

"Damn."

He looked up.

Battle stared back down and offered Tucker a mocking salute.

"Get them!" roared the sergeant, stepping over the injured men.

Battle pulled himself out of the skylight. Keilty was already at the edge of the roof, a small wooden case in his hand. McDonald was balanced on another rooftop. He waved them on.

The officers reached the top landing. They charged for

the door. The officer, whom Battle had poleaxed, was trying to rise, a mouth full of blood, he was groping for balance.

Battle slid down a roof and leapt onto another building. He landed in a heap, moaning. Keilty turned back and urged him to hurry.

An old bed and a wardrobe blocked the door to the attic room. The furniture moved slightly as the door was hit from the other side.

In the street below, Reeves was growing impatient. He looked at the landlord and the other people detained in the raid.

He tapped his watch. He looked across to the junction, where Sir Charles's car was waiting.

Reeves's earlier calm was cracking.

"What's taking so long?" the Inspector turned to a nearby constable. "Get in there. Find Sergeant Tucker and find out what's happening."

The wardrobe and the narrow bed finally gave and a police officer forced his way in. The only light in the room was from the skylight. The bed and wardrobe were pushed aside. Sergeant Tucker barged in. One look was enough. "Thompson, May, Sims. The roof. Beattie, downstairs to the Inspector. Tell him they're on the roof. Move it man. Ryan, Hollis, get out there," Tucker ran his hand over his face. Someone was going to pay for this and Tucker suspected he knew who it was going to be.

The sergeant began to move back out of the small attic room.

"You two, stay there," he snapped.

As Tucker emerged from the attic room, he spared a thought for the young constable, who was fingering a loose tooth. His expression tightened. He stepped up to the smashed balcony.

Tucker's frustration burst.

"They're on the roof. Get out and fan out. Now!" he shouted.

He looked again at the injured constable. The young policeman looked up at him and grimaced.

Tucker's expression softened slightly.

"We'll get them, son."

Chapter Six

Council of War

McDonald shimmied down a drainpipe. He looked up. Keilty's head appeared above him, gauging the drop. He swung a leg over the edge.

Police officers were dashing out of the *Bull and Bush*. The Inspector looked flustered. He pointed at the prison wagon.

Reeves was shouting orders wildly now.

"Get them out of here! Spread out!"

He turned to another officer.

"Get on to the station. We need to close this area off."

The Inspector turned as Sergeant Tucker appeared. Behind him, an officer was bleeding profusely, helped along by his colleagues.

Reeves slapped his cane against his leg.

"Ruddy hell."

The Commissioner looked at his watch. He was still seated in the vehicle with Sir Charles.

"It would seem the birds have flown, Sir Charles."

Sir Charles was slowly fingering his cane. He looked up at the Commissioner.

His stare was dark, his words hung with threat.

"These men are our only clue. The state opening of Parliament is only a week away. What do you think will happen when the king fails to wear the Imperial State Crown then?

"Reputations are won and lost in times like these, Commissioner."

Battle dropped to the ground with a dull thud. He was breathing heavily and rubbing his back. McDonald and Keilty looked at him balefully.

Mac stood over the stocky Londoner.

"Think with your feet in future, not your fists."

Battle pulled a face. He looked at Keilty for support and got none.

McDonald looked about to say more, but changed his mind.

"Right. Let's get out of here."

The trio turned as a milk cart rounded the corner. They froze. They knew they could not afford to be seen.

"Holy…" Keilty glanced at the others.

Battle gave Keilty and Mac a smile.

"Ever hijacked a milk cart?" He chuckled ready to launch himself at the milkman.

The three waited, as the cart, pulled by one horse, approached. The trio tensed.

Keilty spoke quietly.

"He's bound to remember three men at this hour of the morning."

McDonald nodded.

As the cart drew up and stopped, the milkman hailed them.

"Lovely day for going Absent Without Leave."

Shock, then relief, in quick succession, registered on the others' faces. Thomas grinned at their astonishment.

Thomas's orders were quick and decisive.

"Mac, you hop in. You two can walk. Two streets down there's a bus depot. Get on whichever bus is leaving. The first one. We'll meet tonight. At your nephew's place, Tommy," he said.

Battle was still trying to recover from Thomas's appearance.

"Jack's place. Right."

McDonald climbed on to the cart, but Keilty did not move.

"One more thing, Doubtin'. Have you got any change for the bus?"

Thomas scowled. He dug and threw them a coin. Keilty caught it and bit it, as Thomas led the cart away. Battle and Keilty turned and walked the other away. The cart moved on.

"Where are you going?" asked Mac as he climbed aboard.

"Relax. You and I need to talk. Put the overall on. You're sitting on it."

The cart swung around the corner, as McDonald hauled on the clothing. Policemen were running further down the road. Inspector Reeves was standing at the police car talking rapidly to the occupants. The Inspector turned and watched the slow moving milk cart for a moment.

Nothing unusual in that. Reeves turned back to the confusion behind him.

The cart began to turn away from the *Bull and Bush* junction, but McDonald had questions.

"How did you know?"

Thomas shook his head.

"Later."

McDonald risked a quick glance back at the frantic activity surrounding the pub.

Two police officers were walking at the side of the road. The milk cart drew level with them and Thomas leaned out of his cab.

"What's all the commotion about, officer?" His voice a London drawl.

The older constable pointed up the street.

"Escaped convicts."

Thomas looked impressed.

"Hope you catch 'em, son."

The officers nodded back and continued their walk. McDonald looked across at Thomas. Thomas looked back nonchalantly.

"I won't tell you again, RSM McDonald. Get those whiskers off, else you'll wind up back in the Bloody Tower," Thomas's words were darkly Welsh.

★ ★ ★

Two men were hauling a weight out from the dark water of the Thames. They struggled to handle the dead bulk. They pulled it up on to steps that disappeared into the murky river.

The effort to drag it up the steps was considerable. At the top, they let the body fall. It was encased in dark blue. The empty eyes of the dead police constable stared straight past them.

"Christ. It's a Peeler." One turned away to retch.

★ ★ ★

In the warehouse, with the tall shutters pressed closed, work went on under the dull glow of oil lanterns.

The Boers were loading large crates onto a railway carriage. It was back-breaking work, with Sturm directing operations. He stood in the centre of the warehouse drenched in sweat like a foreman in Hell.

Skinstad was the only one not working. He was sitting on a box, smoking and sipping a hot drink from a tin mug.

A shadow fell over him.

Kruger's face was tight, as he dropped a newspaper at Skinstad's feet. Kruger's tone was quizzical, but there were shadows in it.

"Was it necessary?"

Skinstad looked at the paper. 'Policeman murdered in East End'.

Skinstad shrugged.

"I dumped him in the river. The current should have taken him miles away."

Kruger's stare was iron. Hard and brutal.

"It did. Otherwise we wouldn't be having this conversation."

Kruger turned away. Skinstad raised his tin mug in a mocking toast. Sensing trouble, Van Sturm looked across at Skinstad. Van Sturm knew he would have to keep an eye on that one.

★ ★ ★

Thomas was leaning back against the low railing of a majestic bandstand. The brightly-coloured round, wooden structure sat comfortably in the middle of a small lush park. A picturesque playground for the gentry. It was a tranquil, almost sleepy, setting.

There was nothing relaxed about Mac. He was pacing furiously, walking in circles as he spoke; his words rough.

"It canna be. You're talking rubbish. He saved my life. Got the DSO." The Distinguished Service Order was awarded to officers for courage in combat.

McDonald was shaking his head as he prowled.

McDonald stopped and faced his friend.

"No. You've read a few historical, hysterical reports from 26 years ago and got hysterical yourself. You're clutching at straws, Evan."

Thomas studied McDonald intensely, but his voice was reasoned, cold.

"It all fits. Yes, he saved your life. He had to. He'd led the Boers right onto the Gordons. He needed you. You gave him his cover."

McDonald's face was colouring; hardening.

"No. No. He was riding on when they came over the ridge. He didn't need to come back for me. He could have ridden on and left Robbo and me to hold them off. That's what any other officer would have done. No." Mac planted his feet.

Thomas tried again.

"How long after you had pegged the first two Boers did the others come over the hill? Five minutes, 10 minutes? How long Mac? He is about to leave the two of you, head to your brigade's encampment when the Boers come over the hill. Yes, he could have left you to die, but what if you had lived? Lived to tell, how, in his wake, came 200 Boers.

McDonald rejected this.

"He came back for Robbo and me."

Thomas's face was bleak.

"No. He came back for just one of you, someone who would vouch-safe him. Patch the holes in his story. I've read the reports, Mac.

"Laird said that he was on intelligence gathering for General McIntyre, but McIntyre's entire force was wiped out by snipers, caught in the Veldt.

"Yet Laird pops up, 200 miles away, fresh as a daisy, with a small army of Afrikaners on his tail.

"Think about it. Open your eyes."

Looking out over the wide cultivated parkland, McDonald was reliving the day.

Boer horsemen were streaming over the far ridge.

"Christ, we're cooked." he said.

A shot rang out. Robertson crumpled. Mac raised his rifle and fired back. He bent down, but his colleague was dead.

Laird shouted at McDonald.

"Here McDonald. Hurry man!"

McDonald swung round. Laird was reaching down for him. The officer hauled Mac on to the back of his saddle and kicked his mount forward.

Mac was standing with his head in his hands. He looked across at Thomas; his expression one of near loathing.

"What is it with you?" Mac spat the words.

Thomas stared back.

"I'm right."

McDonald straightened up. It was a faintly menacing movement between these old comrades.

"And I know different. We should be concentrating on finding the jewels, not looking for scapegoats for our own failures."

The two friends stared at each other. Thomas stepped closer.

"And what about his mother being born in South Africa? Does that make no difference to you?"

McDonald's face was granite.

Thomas held up a palm.

"All right, Mac. Have it your way. But remember what I've said. The others have to know."

McDonald snorted.

"They'll laugh in your face."

Thomas was not finished.

"Perhaps, but think on this. How did Laird's horse outrun the Boers, with two on his back?"

Thomas swung away. Mac was left to watch him, as the slender Welshman stepped down from the bright bandstand and walked slowly across the gentle park.

★ ★ ★

In his cramped stuffy office at New Scotland Yard, Reeves was pouring over a map of London, his finger on the southern area of the Thames. Reeves ran through all he had done in the past 24 hours. *There had to be a pattern, there always was; motive and method.*

As he did so, police officers and military policemen were checking freight being loaded on to railway carriages at all the major railway stations: King's Cross, Victoria, Paddington and Waterloo. Smaller stations were also being swept, luggage holds scoured. Every boat moored along the Thames was being boarded and searched.

There was a knock on the door. Reeves came back to the map in front of him.

Sergeant Tucker entered, carrying a piece of paper.

"Come in, Tucker. Any joy?"

Tucker presented the paper to him.

"I think so, sir. I think we've got him."

★ ★ ★

The yard at the rear of the *Lucky Sailor* backed on to the River Thames. It was a narrow strip that demanded privacy. A disused gallows pole stood at the end of the yard. Not long ago, it had been a hanging pub. Crowds had gathered to watch the condemned swing. Hanging had been a form of entertainment washed down with a few drinks.

Keilty, McDonald and Thomas were sitting at a bench, directly beneath the gallows. Their voices were low and strained. Keilty looked up at the gallows and crossed himself.

Battle emerged from the back of the building carrying four gins.

Battle laid down the drinks with a flourish.

"Four London gins. The finest in the world. Here's to us, the Four Ravens!"

McDonald stared across the table at Thomas.

"Shut up, Tommy."

Keilty cast McDonald an eye. Battle, deflated, sat down.

McDonald's concentration was fixed on the Welshman.

"Anything else to say? I thought not. Despite your doubts,

he is our best hope." Mac made his point, shifting his weight forward, like a big cat waiting to pounce.

McDonald scanned the group. Battle nodded back at him. Keilty inclined his head fractionally. Thomas smoked his pipe and considered his friend through the smoke.

"On your own head be it."

McDonald's jaw muscles tightened. He stood up, pulled his coat tighter across his chest and strode away down the passageway, an alley for dark deeds, that ran by the side of the pub.

The other three watched him leave.

Battle looked confused.

"Where's he going?"

Keilty looked at Battle in bemused admiration.

Thomas tapped his pipe.

"One day, Tommy Battle, you'll learn the art of listening."

Chapter Seven

Assassin's Knife

Laird replaced the telephone receiver. He looked thoughtful. The telephone was still a relatively new contraption. For Laird, it was a channel of power, connecting him with some of the most important men of his generation. A modern means of communication still only really accessible by the rich and influential, the men that made Britain.

He studied his own portrait hanging on the opposite wall as he reached across and pulled a cord. A distant bell rang.

Laird rubbed his brow.

Seconds later, the door opened to reveal the towering Campbell. Laird remained staring into the mirror above the fireplace. He did not acknowledge Campbell's arrival.

"Send in Argyle."

★ ★ ★

Battle and Thomas were the only two left sitting out in the pub yard now. The wind had picked up. The yard had darkened as the sun withdrew into the dusk. Battle looked as if he had drunk all the gins.

Thomas puffed on his pipe. His face creased.

Battle roused himself.

"You for another, Doubtin'? Thought not."

Battle headed towards the pub, pushing through a doorway not designed for an ex-soldier with Battle's shoulder width.

Battle smiled at the barman, who obviously remembered him. There were five or six customers in the bar.

As Battle handed over his coins, the door opened and a small ragamuffin pushed his way into the bar with a bag too big for him. It was dragging him down, pulling him to earth.

The boy's gruff voice echoed down the bar.

"Evenin' Standard. Copper killed in East End!"

The couple near the boy took a paper. Battle decided.

"Here, son, I'll take one."

The boy looked up and handed the folded paper to Battle. He tucked it underneath his arm and lifted two gins.

Battle stepped into the dusk carrying the drinks.

"I got you one anyway, Doubtin'. Can't drink alone."

Battle dropped the paper on the bench.

"There you go, something to take your mind off things."

The paper fell open and a sketched face stared up from the front page. 'Police murderer sought'. Battle's likeness peered out at them from the paper.

Battle sank to the bench, like a defeated boxer.

"Blinkin' shoot me," he breathed.

Thomas studied Battle's likeness, then the man himself.

"They probably will."

Thomas reached across and picked up a gin. Silently, he toasted a dumbfounded Battle.

★ ★ ★

As McDonald crossed Montague Street, he glanced further down the road, then checked to kneel and tie his bootlace. All the while, he remained alert. Rising slowly, he seemed satisfied. Yet the gnawing sensation between his shoulders persisted.

McDonald climbed the front steps and rang the doorbell. He looked back across the road as the door opened.

Campbell viewed McDonald with a hint of hostility.

"I've come to see…" but McDonald was not allowed to finish.

"Lord Laird is not at home. He's dining at his club tonight," Campbell told him.

McDonald digested this.

"Will you tell him that…"

Campbell interrupted again.

"… Regimental Sergeant Major McDonald called."

Campbell closed the door into Mac's growing frown. McDonald turned away.

He was not beaten yet.

"The Guards' club, Horseguards."

McDonald walked down the steps and turned briskly left. As he did so, a figure detached itself from the shadows across the road. McDonald had a shadow.

★ ★ ★

In the elegant drawing room of the Guards' club, Laird sat with Viscount Crombie, port glasses in their hands.

The Viscount was shaking his head.

"We almost had them."

Laird studied his glass. His cane rested against his knee.

Crombie was in his cups. A sorry state brought on by the rich, red port and the failure to catch the four yeoman warders.

"What puzzles me is how they did it? But we'll find out soon enough," he grumbled.

Laird leaned forward to top up his companion's glass.

That perked up the Viscount.

"It'll all come out at the court martial. Once we've found them and recovered the jewels." He took a sip.

Laird put his glass down.

Laird's tone was an enquiring one, a voice of wise counsel.

"Court martial? Is that wise?"

Laird let his words sink in.

"Have you ever brought down a stag, M'Lord?"

The civil servant listened transfixed. He gulped at his port. Laird was thinking aloud for his companion.

"This ringleader, this, what did you say his name was?"

"McDonald of the Gordons. Bounder got the Military Medal at Ypres."

Laird took a thoughtful, appreciative sip from his glass.

★ ★ ★

McDonald walked purposefully along a narrow winding path, a short cut through St James's Park. In the dark, his ears had become his best defence. He heard a slight noise. Perhaps it was nothing, but that feeling between his shoulder blades screamed caution. That feeling had kept him alive before. He glanced around, but kept walking. A few paces on he stopped. This time he had heard something. In the distance, a busier London could dimly be seen and heard.

McDonald turned back and froze. A dark figure was standing six or seven feet in front of him. In the moonlight, the man raised a cruel curved blade. McDonald looked from the exotic curved knife to the man's eyes. An assassin's eyes. The man readied himself. McDonald looked desperately right and left and came to a decision. He prepared to charge and take his chances. His assailant flashed the knife. McDonald stepped back, measuring the distance between him and the knife. The man's eyes searched McDonald's as his head moved almost in slow motion.

Slowly, like a broken puppet lowered by strings, the man sank to his knees. He twisted, his knife arm folding beneath him, cushioning his fall. He hit the ground surprisingly softly. McDonald looked from the prone figure to another emerging behind the fallen man.

"Evening, Mac. Nice night for stroll. Doubtin' thought you might be needing of a little company," Keilty's voice was quiet, but it carried across the dark park.

McDonald nodded slowly, as though he had been confronted by a revelation.

Keilty prodded the corpse.

"Know him?"

Keilty reached down and extracted his slim, straight blade. Argyle's face stared up at them and the moon.

"No, but I know his master."

Keilty weighed the sikh blade in his hand.

Keilty turned to practical considerations. "We'll put him in the…"

McDonald nodded, a fierce look on his face, but he was already moving.

"No rash moves, Mac. Doubtin' asked me to make sure you got home safely."

There was no misunderstanding the command in Keilty's voice.

McDonald stared at the Irish hitman, struggled to control himself, and consented.

★ ★ ★

Inspector Reeves sat studying the sketch of Tommy Battle. He reached for his cup, but the contents were cold.

Reeves pulled a face.

"Hinchcliffe!"

There was the hurried sound of movement from outside the office. The door opened, a tired-looking officer, Constable Hinchcliffe, stuck his head around the door.

Reeves looked tired too, but rank permitted him to be angry and short.

"This tea's cold."

Hinchcliffe nodded and closed the door.

★ ★ ★

A Hackney carriage drew up outside Laird's residence. Laird's cane was followed by the man, as he stepped out. He paid off the cabbie and stood watching it disappear down the street. Laird scanned the still road. He walked up the stairs.

The door opened as he reached the top step. Laird entered without breaking his stride.

Campbell took Laird's hat, coat and gloves, but Laird kept his cane. He looked at his manservant.

"No news, Campbell?"

"None, sir."

Laird gave a slight stiff nod.

Chapter Eight

A New Enemy

The *Lucky Sailor* was in gloom, shrouded in stillness.

Battle and his nephew, Jack, were sitting with a couple of empty glasses in front of them. The barman, Ted, was clearing away empties. There was a rattle on the side door. Everyone looked up. Two knocks, a pause, two more. Jack nodded to Ted, who walked around the bar and pulled back the bolts. Mac and Keilty slipped inside.

Battle studied their faces.

"Dirty work, eh, comrades?"

McDonald and Keilty hauled off their coats. Jack signalled Ted.

"A bottle and two more glasses, if you please, Ted," said Jack.

The new arrivals sat, as Ted returned with the bottle and glasses.

Battle laughed.

"You might as well join us, Ted. You're already in it up to your eyeballs."

McDonald reached for the drink, waited for Ted to return with his glass and poured. Everyone watched his hand. McDonald's smile was a twist as he realised they were watching him. His hands were steady as granite.

The five drank. McDonald poured another.

"Well?" asked Battle.

McDonald's words were harsh and bitter.

"Doubtin' was right. Argyle. Laird's man. He'd have stuffed me like a duck, but for Gerard."

There was no reaction from the Irishman.

Jack looked between the two old soldiers.

"Where is he now?" Jack asked.

McDonald held Jack's gaze.

"Swimming in the Serpentine."

Ted and Jack exchanged anxious confirming glances. Battle chortled.

Suddenly, Battle was serious.

"What I want to know is why? Why a peer of the realm would be involved. Why? Has he gone off his rocker?"

"Perhaps you should tell us, Mac." The drinkers all spun round, stunned.

Thomas glided out from the shadows at the end of the bar.

They all look startled. Thomas only had eyes for McDonald. The Scotsman stared back.

His mind was back in the Veldt.

McDonald and Robertson watched Major Laird spur his horse away.

Robertson patted MacDonald on the arm.

"Reckon he owes you one, Mac. There'll be tin in it for you."

McDonald watched Laird.

"One of Scotland's finest, Robbo. Major Magnus Laird. My father kent him."

Robertson was distracted.

"NO!" he shouted his warning.

Boer horsemen were streaming over the far ridge.

McDonald spied them, too.

"Damn, we're cooked."

A shot rang out. Robertson crumpled. He pitched forward. Mac raised his rifle and fired back. The leading Boer horseman was punched out of his saddle. McDonald bent down, but his colleague was dead. A gaping bullet hole in his back. Mac put his hand on it and began to turn in the direction that Laird had just ridden off in.

Laird's voice was urgent.

"Here, McDonald. Hurry man!"

McDonald swung round. Laird was reaching down for him. The officer hauled McDonald onto the back of his saddle and kicked his mount forward.

McDonald broke eye contact with Thomas and looked at his glass. He turned it in his hand. He cast his glance at Battle and Keilty. Acceptance washed over him.

"Laird. He shot Robbo."

Keilty looked on with compassion. Battle poured Mac another measure.

McDonald was struggling with his memories.

"Robbo was hit in the back. He was facing the Boers, raising his rifle. The bullet took him in the back. Laird shot him.

"Doubtin's right. Laird only came back for me. When he came over the ridge, the Boers were too close. They could have winged him. He was WITH them."

McDonald gulped down the whisky.

The others looked to Thomas. He took his time, like an experienced storyteller.

"Laird's entire company was wiped out at Van Tonders Nek on August 6. He had been reported missing in action, presumed dead. Eighteen days before the attack at Ladysmith.

"Later, he was to claim Colonel Peterson, General Roberts's old spymaster, had given him a special intelligence role, skirting behind the Boers. No such order had been written down. Peterson had given it on August 5.

"Who would doubt Laird's word? Ask Peterson? He was dead, killed with the rest of them at Waschbank River. But Laird survived.

"Survived and was leading a large force of Boers for a surprise attack at Bulwana Mountain."

Thomas walked across from the bar. He poured Mac

another shot and filled himself one. Veins stood out in his neck.

Thomas concentrated on Mac's face.

"If you and Robertson hadn't been there, an entire brigade would have been wiped out. They would have had no warning. Between you, you ruined the attack and saved the Gordons from slaughter."

McDonald looked miles away. His hand tightened on the glass.

Keilty's voice was a whisper.

"So he changed his plan."

Thomas nodded.

"Yes, who would doubt an officer who had ridden back to save the life of a ranker?

Thomas sat down.

"Laird came back for Mac. An insurance policy. He couldn't take a chance and simply leave Robertson. He might have survived and what then?

"No. Mac was his banker."

Battle wiped his mouth.

"Blimey. A ruddy peer of the realm."

Thomas was not finished.

"A highly decorated, highly respected officer, a leading politician and gentleman. And on the death of his father and, later, his older brother in a shooting accident, a member of the House of Lords."

McDonald's face tightened.

Thomas had McDonald's attention.

"Did he take a special interest in your progress, Mac? Nurture your loyalty."

McDonald's fingers tightened on his glass.

Thomas was relentless.

"Turn out every time you got some tin. Put in a good word for you as you earned your promotions," the Welshman was intense.

Keilty laid his hand on Mac's arm, as Battle began to pour Mac another drink. Mac brushed him off violently. The Scot stared at Thomas.

"You're saying he bought me." There was violence in McDonald's voice.

Thomas shook his head slowly, sadly.

Thomas laid his hands on the table in front of the Scot.

"No, RSM John Cameron McDonald, you have earned every rank and citation that you have. That and more, and I am proud to have known you and served with you."

McDonald struggled with himself.

"Laird worked to keep your loyalty. Worked to keep your memory of the event blurred with gratitude."

McDonald's face twisted.

"I'm going to kill him."

"Not before we get the jewels back." Thomas met McDonald's statement with steel. Sharp and dangerous.

Chapter Nine

Gold in Hand

The railway depot was deserted. Engines and stock positioned for the night, forming solid blocks of shadow.

A small, stubby engine pulled in a couple of freight wagons. The train was moving very slowly, less than walking pace. A man dropped from the engine platform. It was Kruger. His eyes searched out the still railway yard.

Someone was watching. Only his black polished boots visible in the shadows.

The train stopped. Kruger walked along the platform. He looked tense as he approached a small hut.

Skinstad stepped out of the shadow with another young Boer, Janni, thin but muscled. Kruger's eyes narrowed.

"All clear?"

"Clear," confirmed Skinstad.

Kruger was not satisfied.

"What about the watchmen?"

"Taken care of."

Kruger weighed this up.

"Nothing rash, I hope."

Skinstad nodded to his colleague.

"Janni put enough 'chloro' in their tea urn to fell a wildebeest. They've been snoring like pigs for an hour."

Kruger nodded to Janni.

"Where's Halle?"

Skinstad jerked his head.

"Lookout. Just in case we have any visitors."

Kruger nodded, satisfied this time.

"Right."

Kruger scanned the yard again.

Inside the railway guardroom, three railway watchmen were slumped in their chairs. Two with heads in hands, another with his head lolling back.

A sleek powerful steam engine, the *Highland Spirit*, stood gleaming under the arc lights.

★ ★ ★

Laird's residence was in shadow.

The lord was sitting deep in his armchair, his fingers twisting the wolf's head of his cane. Restless, he pulled out his watch.

"Argyle should have reported back by now."

Laird lay his timepiece on the coffee table and lifted his whisky glass. He took a sip, trying to wash away his mounting anxiety.

★ ★ ★

Inspector Reeves's office looked as if he had lived there for a week with papers strewn on every surface. His clothes and face crumpled and tired, Reeves sat forward, his fingers rubbing his already bloodshot eyes. In front of him was a piece of paper with words scrawled out: 'Tower', 'McDonald', 'Battle', 'Keilty', 'Docks'.

A sharp rap on the door brought Reeves out of his thoughts.

"Yes?"

Hinchcliffe, looking equally tired, stuck his head around the door.

"This just came in, sir. Straight from Downing Street, sir."

Hinchcliffe was nervous.

The Inspector took the envelope and tore it open. He read it, then he read it again.

"Call me a car, Hinchcliffe."

"There's one waiting, sir."

Reeves reached for his overcoat.

A black car of officialdom turned into Westminster Square, arcing round into Whitehall.

The Inspector and Commissioner sat nervously as the car swung into Downing Street. Neither looked pleased despite the luxury of the fine leather upholstery.

★ ★ ★

Inside the cavernous shunting yard, Sturm looked back down towards the freight wagons. He signalled and his driver edged the engine backwards.

Skinstad stood on the platform next to a railway carriage. He signalled to Sturm as the freight wagons were pushed backwards.

The freight wagon coupled with the carriages with a dull clang. Skinstad jumped down and checked the link and turned to give Sturm the thumbs up.

Two spots of light appeared in the distant gloom. Heavy boots echoed down the platform. Two night watchmen moved slowly towards the depot doors.

One checked the padlocked door. Kruger watched from a recess. One of the watchmen stopped near the door as if he had heard something.

Kruger tensed.

The watchman shrugged, nodded to his colleague and the pair walked off. Kruger slipped his knife back into its sheath, breathing out slowly as he did so.

Sturm, sweating heavily, turned to clap his driver on the back. The stoker, Pieter, gleaming with effort, smiled at the beefy Sturm.

Kruger, on the platform with Janni, nodded at Skinstad and Sturm. All was going to plan.

* * *

In a small, surprisingly understated drawing room in Downing Street, the two senior police officers were standing waiting. The door opened admitting Sir Charles, bristling with energy.

"Gentlemen, you can add this character to your list."

The civil servant handed over a file to the policemen. Marked on it was a single name 'EVAN HORATIO THOMAS, DCM'.

* * *

Deep in the shadows of the *Lucky Sailor*, a council of war was in progress. Another bottle had appeared on the table. These men had soldiered all over the world. Fought and drank and fought again when they had lived to tell the tale. The set of faces was hard. Only Keilty was sitting back in his seat, a languid, casual demeanour.

Thomas's annoyance was aimed at Jack.

"Why didn't you speak earlier, Jack?"

Jack looked back abashed. He shrugged.

"I was too wrapped up. What with everything, Lord Laird an' all. The revelations."

He indicated McDonald slightly, but the Scot did not blink. Jack was faintly nervous.

"I got news a few hours ago. There's a warehouse.

Rotherhithe way. Been empty for donkeys. Well, until a week ago."

"Where?" interrupted Battle.

"The haberdashers' old Russian place."

Battle nodded.

Thomas assumed command.

"Tommy, you and Mac check the warehouse. Ged and I will tackle Laird."

McDonald's muscles in his face tightened, but Thomas was not finished.

"Jack, we need armour: a revolver each, a couple of shotguns and a couple of Enfields and plenty of ammo. Tommy, start growing a 'tash. Jack, we need a pair of glasses for him, with plain glass," Thomas pointed at Battle.

Jack nodded.

"Can do."

"And get him a heavy cap. His face is more famous than Charlie Chaplin's at the moment."

Battle looked embarrassed, but Thomas was taking no prisoners.

"Ted, you stay here and handle any messages."

"Remember, the only lead the authorities have is us. We are the hunters and the hunted."

Keilty seemed curiously pleased.

"Cry havoc and let loose the Dogs of War."

They all nodded, strangely satisfied, as Keilty poured them a final drink.

★ ★ ★

The Commissioner and Inspector sat in silence as they were driven back to New Scotland Yard. The Inspector had Thomas's file in his hands.

However, Reeves looked uncertain.

"Do you really think they did it, sir?"

The Commissioner stirred and turned from looking out of the window.

"Find them, Reeves. Find them. Find the jewels."

The Inspector studied his superior, who had given him no answer.

* * *

Keilty was watching the front door of Laird's majestic townhouse. He looked back down the street. A cab was parked 30 yards away.

He looked back across the road. The door opened and Laird stood taking in the morning air.

He trotted down the steps and looked up and down for a cab. Laird signalled the cab parked down the road, but the driver appeared to be asleep. Laird made no effort to hide his annoyance. He looked the other way. Nothing. A cab turned into view from the other direction. Laird strode out into the street, raising his cane.

Laird climbed into the cab, barking muffled instructions as it moved off. Keilty watched it go. He turned to step into another cab as it drew up. Thomas, the cab driver, touched his cap to his passenger and the cab moved off, matching the leading cab's pace.

* * *

Euston station was busy. The newspaper vendors were already at work. Porters hauled leather luggage onto rough-hewed wooden carts. Queues snaked out from the ticket booths. The entire cavernous station concourse smelled of steam, oil and damp coal. Police and the occasional military policeman were standing at corners, positioned to cover the exits. Among them was the bulky shape of Sergeant Tucker, scanning the crowd.

"It's the docks we should be concentrating on," his words carried to a young constable standing next to him, but he knew better than to speak. Tucker's humour had evaporated since the debacle at the *Bull and Bush*.

★ ★ ★

Battle and McDonald stood looking up at the haberdashers' old Russian warehouse. Disused, it was still an imposing building. Tall, with two sets of wide wooden doors that operated on rollers. Cut into the doors were smaller ones, just large enough for a man to step through. A building designed to hold huge quantities of goods that could be shunted in and out by train. They walked cautiously towards it. Both scanned the old brick building. Their eyes swept the mammoth doors and long windows for signs of movement.

McDonald and Battle considered the chained lock of the warehouse. McDonald nodded to Battle as a set of skeleton keys appeared in the Londoner's hands.

The sound of the keys being tested in the lock carried in the still dawn air. Three keys later and Battle gave a satisfied grin.

The huge sliding doors were pulled open. Mac and Battle were silhouetted in the opening of the warehouse.

McDonald and Battle stood a few feet into the building, becoming accustomed to the darkness. Mac nodded past Battle. Taking his cue, the Londoner moved in the other direction.

★ ★ ★

Sitting bolt upright in the taxi, Laird looked tense. He was twisting his cane between his gloved fingers, as the cab flashed past London streets. Laird stared straight ahead, impatient to reach his destination.

Forty yards further down the street, Thomas manoeuvred his cab behind the one carrying Laird. Although tense, Thomas was enjoying his role as a cabbie. His taxi, a dark green Beardmore Mk I, had been selected to blend in. Thomas watched the cab ahead and smiled, Laird's cab was the new fangled black. *It would never catch on – stood out like a shiner.*

Laird's cab turned down a street.

Thomas moved quickly to follow.

"Where the blazes is he going?" Thomas muttered to himself.

* * *

Small groups of railwaymen trudged into the railway depot, lunch tins slung over their shoulders as they clocked in to start the morning shift.

An engine driver, Alf, polished his bald head with one hand as he walked up the platform. He reached the engine, the *Highland Spirit*.

The stoker, Paul, a bent muscular figure, was shovelling coal into the furnace.

Alf hauled himself up.

"How's tricks, Paulie?"

Paul grunted.

"The miserable git wants to see yer. In his office."

Alf hung up his knap sack and nodded.

"That's all I need."

Alf jumped down from the polished engine plate and plodded towards the ticket barrier. Beyond it, he spied Bert, the miserable git in question, a tall, peaky-looking night watchman. Bert was standing near the door to their mess room. Alf sauntered up to him, ready for an argument.

"Yes, Bert. What was you after?" Alf's tone was insolent.

"Everything kosher, Alf?"
Alf frowned slightly.
"Yeah. Why? You look like death, Bert."
Bert looked worse.
"We've all got it. Sick as dogs all night"
"Well, you look like it, mate. Like death," said Alf.
Alf turned away and walked up the platform. A satisfied smile grew on his face with every step.

★ ★ ★

Battle moved slowly through the warehouse. The shutters on the ground floor windows were all bolted closed. Squares of irregular light from the shutterless upper windows gave the warehouse floor a patched-work effect; blocks of light creating a giant chessboard. Battle was whistling *Greensleeves* softly. He stopped. He bent down and picked up a rough sack from a pile dumped against a row of crates.

"Mac!"

Mac looked across and stepped forward. Something caught on his foot. He went down on one knee and reached out. His fingers met a railway track. Mac edged forward through a wall of shadow.

Battle was kneeling by a footprint of a heavy army boot.

"Curiouser and curiouser. Mac!"

Mac appeared above him.

Battle looked up.

"All the prints are the same. Lots of them. The sacks could have been used to carry the jewels over the Tower walls. They could have been loaded into these."

Battle pointed to a stack of crates. Burnt on to their sides were the words 'Fragile Antiques'.

"What do you reckon? And I found these in the office over there."

The clothing in Battle's hand was pitch black, the same as worn by Kruger and his team.

Mac nodded and slowly opened his palm. In the middle of it was a gold doubloon. Battle's eyes widened. Mac nodded.

"They were here. Shipped the stuff out by rail."

Mac pointed to the railway lines heading towards the huge double door at the far end of the warehouse.

"Keep looking. There may be something."

Battle rose. Mac clenched the gold coin. He flicked it up into the air and caught it. His eyes were alive.

Chapter Ten

Imports and Exports

Laird's cab pulled up in front of the Natural History Museum.

"At last," Thomas muttered, angling his vehicle to pull up a cab's length behind Laird's.

As Laird climbed out of the cab, Thomas tapped the glass passenger partition window. Keilty jumped out, looking to Thomas. Perched in his cab, Thomas motioned ahead, as Laird climbed the wide stone steps.

Keilty watched Laird.

"He's meeting someone."

Thomas agreed.

Keilty took stock.

"Best we both go in. You stay on him, I'll follow his rendezvous," said the Irishman, stepping away from the cab.

Thomas nodded as he watched Keilty turn to tail Laird.

★ ★ ★

Inspector Reeves looked haggard. He was more of a mess than his office. A small bottle of brandy sat next to him. He was staring at the files on his desk. He ran his fingers through his hair, picking up Thomas's file.

The policeman was running over what was before him. He'd done this countless times, waiting for the pattern to emerge.

"Decorated. Distinction. Bravery."

He dropped that file and picked up Battle's.

"MM and Bar. One of Kitchener's favourites."

He looked at the likeness between the sketch of Battle and his record picture.

Reeves shook his head, nothing fitted.

"These men are heroes. Heroes."

The Inspector stood up and pulled on his coat. *When in doubt, act.*

★ ★ ★

South of the river others were also looking for clues. Battle was still searching the warehouse. He stooped, making a find.

"Mac! Here!"

Mac turned back towards Battle's low voice.

Battle looked pleased, as he pointed to the side of a crate tilted amid the remains of a small fire. It was blank. Mac frowned. Battle's grin widened as he raised a stamp and hammered it onto the frame. The imprint read *Messrs. Hodges and Horillo, Importers and Exporters*. Mac's eyes bored into the words. His fingers tightened on the coin.

★ ★ ★

Laird, his hands resting on his cane, was standing in front of 'Tyrannosaurus Rex', one of the centrepieces of the Natural History Museum. It was part of the most magnificent collection of dinosaur skeletons in the world. Laird appeared to be studying the creature's powerful jaws.

"That's what the Empire has become, Amon Kruger, a dinosaur."

The Afrikaner took a sharp intake of breath. He looked uncomfortable with Laird using his name, but Laird was oblivious.

"Soon, it, too, shall be extinct."

Kruger's eyes narrowed.

"Extinct. Yes. When you proposed this… It can be done. The British Empire humiliated. Stripped of pride," said Kruger.

Laird came out of his reverie.

"We have a problem."

Kruger was surprised and slightly uneasy.

"All went smoothly."

Laird turned his attention to the ancient bones casting a shadow over them.

"The warder at the Tower, McDonald. Your man didn't kill him. He knows you're Boers. He and two other yeoman warders went AWOL. They are looking for you.

"I have taken certain steps. The authorities are looking for them, but it would be better if they do not find them."

Kruger's scar was livid.

"Warders? From the Tower? These are old men…"

Laird did not let him finish.

"These are the cream of the British Army. They all fought in South Africa. Probably everywhere else in the world." Laird's tone was icy.

"One of them, McDonald, is the Gordon Highlander, the man who killed your father on the ridge at Bulwana.

"McDonald." Kruger was still with quiet, a killer statue.

Laird tapped his cane.

"Shot him out of his saddle before I could intervene."

Laird shot a glance at Kruger to check he had his attention. Muscles worked along Kruger's jaw-line.

"Report." Laird's voice snapped at Kruger.

Kruger pulled himself out of shock with difficulty.

"The goods will leave London in two hours. The rendezvous is set."

"Good."

"What of McDonald?"

Laird smiled, but, angled beside him, Kruger could not see Laird's expression and its cruelty.

"Steps have been taken." Laird seemed dangerously calm.

"Steps? What..."

Laird's cane tip struck the floor.

"Leave me two men. I'll deal with McDonald and his merry band." Kruger's eyes burned into Laird, but the peer was unfazed. He stood studying the giant skeleton before him, as Kruger wheeled away, striding down the hall. Keilty stepped away from an exhibit and followed.

Laird remained staring up at the skeleton, transfixed. Little more than 30 feet away, Thomas was watching him.

"I'd like to drop you right now, M'Lord," whispered Thomas, his hand brushing where his weapon was concealed in his waistband.

Kruger emerged through the museum's large wooden doors. He stopped at the top of the steps, running his fingers along his scarred cheek. Kruger walked briskly down the steps and into the street. Keilty came out from the building and followed him. The Irishman's gait was leisurely, while Kruger strode down the street. Keilty was still trailing him. Kruger kept walking. The South African stopped in front of an underground station. He glanced backwards. No sign of Keilty. To Kruger's right, leaning against the station wall was the Irishman. His face obscured by the newspaper he was reading. 'Body found in Serpentine' read the headline.

Kruger looked at his wristwatch. Disquieted, he moved on. Keilty handed the paper to someone passing, who nodded his surprised gratitude. Keilty smiled fractionally and walked after Kruger.

★ ★ ★

A cab drew up in front of Laird's townhouse, allowing Laird to clamber out. Another cab passed as he did so and Thomas watched the lord climb the steps to his residence. Thomas pulled his cab into the kerb and waited.

The two police officers, Inspector Reeves and Sergeant Tucker stood uncomfortably in Laird's study. Lord Laird was seated in his armchair. He regarded them balefully.

Inspector Reeves cleared his throat.

"Well, M'Lord. We won't detain you any longer. Thank you for your assistance." Reeves's nervousness showed.

"Thank *you*, Inspector, for taking the trouble to come and deal with this matter personally."

The Inspector nodded.

He gathered his courage under Laird's pale blue eyes.

"One final matter, sir. We just wanted to know what you'd like doing with the body, M'Lord."

Laird's eyes were cold, but his voice quiet and mild.

"Argyle had no blood family. Campbell and I were his family. Have the body delivered here, Inspector."

The officers looked uncertain, but under Laird's powerful gaze they wilted.

"Of course, sir, as you wish."

The police officers, feeling themselves dismissed, nodded and turned away. They were at the door when Laird stirred to speak again.

"Inspector. Were there any signs of a struggle?"

The officers stopped.

Inspector Reeves checked, hesitating slightly.

"No, sir. Some coward knifed him in the back. Besides that, not a mark on him, sir. The only strange thing is that his wallet was still on him. The thieves must have been disturbed, M'Lord."

Laird nodded slowly as his hand turned the wolf's headed

cane. He was deep in thought as the officers trudged out.

Laird looked to the servants' bell, but Campbell appeared without him even reaching for it.

"Shall I pack for you, Sahib?"

Laird nodded deliberately.

His mind was elsewhere. Back in time, remembering when Argyle first joined his service.

"Campbell, tell that insolent cook that we will be away for some time."

Campbell nodded and turned away.

"Campbell!"

The manservant stopped.

"When did Argyle join us?"

"India, '89. With us since then, Sir."

"With us in China," said Laird.

Campbell did not answer.

"Knew the Oriental techniques, didn't he?"

"Yes, sir."

Laird's nod was a knowing one.

"Whoever killed him must have been very good, Campbell. Very quiet and very quick."

Laird turned his cane.

"Expect two visitors tonight."

Outside Laird's house, Thomas watched as the two police officers stood looking somewhat out of place on Laird's doorstep.

The two officers glanced back at the imposing door behind them. A world once again closed to them.

Sergeant Tucker cleared his throat.

"Begging your pardon, sir, but he didn't seem too upset. Nor surprised neither."

"He's a war hero, Sergeant. Hardened to it."

But Reeves's face said something different.

★ ★ ★

Kruger walked across the concourse at Euston station. Keilty paused at the south entrance, watching.

In the centre of the busy railway station, Kruger halted beneath a large clock. He checked his watch before turning towards the ticket office.

He looked left and right, noting the number of police constables and military police. Again he consulted his watch. He paused again, as if sensing something.

Keilty entered the station. He, too, noted the men in uniforms. He pulled his cap further down and moved slowly through the crowd. There was no sign of Kruger, causing a flicker of concern on Keilty's face.

Kruger walked down the crowded platform past the engine of the regal *Highland Spirit*. Kruger passed two police officers. They noted his scar, but paid him no further attention. He sauntered past a passenger carriage, with Skinstad seated at the window.

Keilty moved along the entrances to the platforms, scanning for Kruger, reading the destination signs as he did so.

His frown was growing.

Kruger moved along the platform, before climbing into a carriage. Moments later, two figures jumped down from the carriage that Kruger had just climbed onto. Both were young, fit men, with strong walks. One of them was Janni. The other, Halle, bore a pockmarked face.

Keilty lit a cigarette. He scanned the crowd and spied Janni and Halle heading out of the station. He nodded as if making a decision, sidestepped two police officers and followed the two Boers.

★ ★ ★

Laird was sitting in his drawing room, sipping sherry. His face was drawn, as he studied the clock on the mantle, 3pm, and compared it with his own silver timepiece. His smile was cold and triumphant.

One hundred yards from Laird's residence, Thomas was dozing in the cab when Keilty rapped on the door.

"Wake up, old timer."

Thomas jerked upright.

"I wasn't asleep."

Keilty looked at him.

"I lost him, Evan."

Thomas lost control.

"Hell and damnation!"

Keilty looked calmer.

"Scarface left Laird two minders."

Keilty nodded towards Laird's house. Janni and Halle were walking up the steps. The door opened and Campbell towered over the young Boers, beckoning them to enter.

Thomas smiled crookedly.

"Reinforcements. You stay on Laird. If he makes a move stick with him and, Ged, he may be our only lead."

★ ★ ★

A clerk, Mr Timms, a dapper man with a small moustache, was filling in a ledger. The offices of *Messrs. Hodges and Horillo, Importers and Exporters* were well established, the walls lined with dark mahogany cabinets; exotic and expensive.

At the ring of a bell, Mr Timms looked up towards the front door. There was no one there. Mr Timms was perplexed. He returned to his books.

A cough.

A startled Mr Timms jolted upright. A well-dressed Thomas looked enquiringly down at him.

Timms recovered.

"Yes, sir?"

Timms noticed another man, with his broad back to him, casting an eye around the small office.

Timms tried again.

"Sir?"

Thomas stuck out his hand.

"Townsley." Thomas's voice betrayed no accent.

He pumped Timm's hand. The clerk grimaced slightly.

"Timms. General Manager."

Thomas nodded, appraising the clerk.

"Mr Timms. My colleague and I are considering using your firm for a forthcoming business venture. We hope that this venture will prove mutually beneficial."

Thomas leaned in.

"Extremely beneficial."

Timms nodded and glanced across at the tall, bear-like figure, who was still prowling. McDonald turned and smiled at him, but that only served to make Timms more nervous.

Thomas indicated the back office. Timms looked again at McDonald. He was torn, but allowed himself to be guided by Thomas into the back office.

"Of course, Mr..."

Thomas gave him an encouraging smile.

"Townsley. With a 'y'."

McDonald continued his scanning of the office.

Thomas sat back in one of the fine leather chairs and signalled that Timms should take a note. Thomas was leaning back further, getting into his role.

"Next month looks most likely. Pending certain details being finalised," Thomas halted to check he had the clerk's full attention.

Timms nodded and looked up. He was startled. McDonald was standing over him, his eyes assessing the room. Mac's eyes focused on a small safe.

Thomas fixed the small man in his sights.

"Would you mind putting your terms in writing, please?"

"Now?"

Thomas smiled. So did Mac.

Chapter Eleven

Enfields, Treason and Plot

Even in the gloom that followed dusk the sign above the door of *Messrs. Hodges and Horillo, Importers and Exporters*, glistened. Pressed into the shadow of the front door of the merchants, Battle and McDonald edged closer to the door. Thomas waited with the cab across the road.

He looked up and down the street. He nodded, urging them to hurry.

Battle pulled out a heavy bunch of skeleton keys. The keys jangled in spite of his care.

Mac nudged him.

"Quiet, man."

Battle tried another key. Mac looked impatient. Battle tried a third key.

"Patience, Mac."

The key slid in and the lock turned. Battle grinned at Mac. McDonald moved forward. Battle checked him then opened the door for him.

"Age before beauty."

Thomas nervously watched them disappear inside.

Inside the inner office, Battle was crouched by the safe, running his gloved hands over it and pursing his lips. He placed a small bag on the floor. McDonald was standing at his shoulder.

Battle looked thoughtful. He pulled up a stethoscope to his ear and listened to the safe just above the combination disc.

Mac cleared his throat. Battle looked up at him and frowned. Mac frowned back and swung away impatiently.

Battle flexed his fingers and gingerly turned the disc.

Another turn. Battle nodded to himself, concentrating deeply.

McDonald's voice was a low husk.

"What's keeping you?"

Battle broke his concentration.

"It's been a long time. I was only 16 or so."

McDonald straightened.

"Well, we haven't got that long."

★ ★ ★

Inside the *George and Dragon*, a large public house frequented by servants and tradesmen, Keilty stood casually at the bar. The barmaid gave him an encouraging smile. Keilty smiled back shyly. He took a sip and glanced around, his ears straining.

"I tell you. Not so much as a by your leave." The voice was indignant, slightly arched. It was a house servant, perhaps a cook, bitter and proud.

Keilty turned and located the voice's source. The cook was a short, dumpy woman, her hair tied back; strands of grey wire.

"He's just upping and flaming well going back up to Scotland."

Cook was sitting with a couple of cronies. Keilty smiled into his beer and angled towards them.

★ ★ ★

The *Highland Spirit* hurtled along. A feat of modern engineering, it could reach speeds of up to 70mph.

Sturm walked along through a busy carriage. He was looking for someone. He reached where Skinstad was sleeping and prodded him, none too gently.

Skinstad jolted awake. Sturm leaned close.

"He wants you."

Skinstad looked surprised, but quickly stood and followed the big man.

★ ★ ★

Outside a small green cabman's shelter, a shadow approached. The hut resembled an overgrown garden shed. There were more than 50 dotted across London. Built through charitable donations to provide a hot meal and shelter to London's cab drivers.

A knock was signalled on the door. Two strikes then two more. The door opened and the shadow swept inside.

Ted stepped back to let in Keilty, the shadow.

Battle, McDonald, Jack and Thomas were clustered around a small narrow table. On the flat wooden surface were four revolvers, a line of knives, four Enfield rifles and boxes of ammunition – a small arsenal. Keilty sat across from them, taking in the narrow confines of the wooden panelled shelter. As was his custom, Keilty sat facing the door. Battle picked one of the Enfields and slipped back the breech.

Thomas looked at Ged.

"Scotland."

Thomas nodded.

"Scotland." Mac nodded.

McDonald passed across the document they had 'acquired' at Hodges and Horillo.

"He's going to Drumgoyne."

Battle's confusion added to his annoyance.

"Where the ruddy hell is that?"

"On the Isle of Glengoyne. Where I was born."

This only added to Battle's bewilderment.

"Isle? You mean?"

McDonald was amused.

"Yes, Tommy, we'll have to get a boat or you can swim."

Battle shook his head.

"Forget that for a game of soldiers."

Keilty and Jack laughed. Thomas smiled at Battle, but Mac, despite the joke, remained serious.

"The wolf is taking the prize to his lair and that is where we are going to trap him."

Mac gripped the doubloon. He flicked it in the air and closed his fist around it.

★ ★ ★

Sturm was leading the way along the locomotive's swaying corridor. He stopped at a carriage door and knocked, opened the door and indicated for Skinstad to go in.

Kruger was sitting in the shadows. Skinstad nodded to him and sat down opposite.

Kruger stared out of the window. Skinstad studied him. He was a touch unnerved. Kruger spoke without looking at Skinstad.

Kruger's voice was low, distant.

"When we took the jewels at the Tower, you failed me."

Skinstad's face tensed, but Kruger forestalled him.

"You fought with a warder. Not a soldier, but an old man. He's still alive."

Skinstad swallowed and picked his next words carefully.

"He fell. It was dark. We didn't have any time. I'd wounded him."

Kruger was contemptuous.

"You scratched him."

Skinstad stared at his commander. Kruger leaned forward,

his scar was revealed. It was ugly, and at this moment, Kruger looked deadly.

"You failed."

Kruger's knife flashed across Skinstad's face. He was left with blood running down his cheek. Skinstad controlled his urge to reach up and touch the wound.

"The man you SCRATCHED. He was at *Bulwana*."

Kruger turned the blade in his hand.

"They hunted us down. We are still the hunted. With the British it is always the same.

"Packing women and children into camps for sickness and starvation to claim them."

Skinstad was grimacing against the pain, but Kruger had not finished.

"I thought about leaving you in London to finish the job, but he knows your face. Perhaps now he wouldn't recognise you.

Skinstad's eyes were black with hate.

Kruger weighed the blade.

"You are on the threshold of death. One wrong step and you will fall." The moment passed.

Kruger smiled.

"Clean yourself up and have Sturm sew you up. He has nimble fingers."

Skinstad stumbled to his feet. He yanked open the door. Kruger wiped his blade and settled back in his seat.

Sturm looked up as Skinstad stepped out of the carriage, a bloodied hand holding his cheek together. Sturm turned away and Skinstad trailed behind.

★ ★ ★

In the narrow wooden taxi hut, weapons were being cleaned. Thomas passed Keilty an Enfield. He smiled and shook his head. On his knees balanced a small wooden briefcase.

Battle pointed to it.

"Didn't figure you for a Mason, Ged."

Keilty flicked open the case. Inside lay the components of a sniper's rifle.

Thomas raised an eyebrow. Mac nodded.

"I wondered why you were hugging that thing when we jumped out of the *Bull and Bush*."

Battle was all admiration.

"Lovely."

Thomas was pleased.

"Well done, Jack. Did you get the other stuff?"

Jack nodded.

"It's all in the bags over there."

Keilty's hands moved over the pieces of the rifle. He snapped it together. Screwed in the barrel, the trigger mechanism, the stock. Finally, slotted on the sights and capped it with a silencer. All this took just a few seconds.

McDonald looked at the Irishman.

"It's been a long time. May I?"

Thomas was handing out canvas sacks and small cases. Battle looked perplexed.

"What the ruddy hell is all this stuff for, Doubtin'?"

McDonald interrupted.

"Shut up and listen, Tommy."

Thomas waited for silence.

"We mustn't attract any attention. Therefore, we can't travel as a group, but we must all be on the train with Laird.

"You…"

Thomas pointed at Mac.

"You, Mac, in particular. You must pretend to get drunk so they put you in the lock up. The rest of us will have other roles to play."

★ ★ ★

Inspector Reeves was at his desk, pouring over a map of London. If possible, Reeves looked even more worn out. He hadn't shaven, his eyes were almost red raw. He traced a heavy lead pencil over the surface of the map. The tip hovered over the Tower of London, then edged south into the area known as London's Docklands. Then the point moved again. One by one, it visited London's main railway stations: Euston, King's Cross, Paddington, Victoria and Waterloo. Reeves was homing in.

★ ★ ★

In the small wooden taxi hut, a head was being shaved. The hair fell around a pair of boots and chair legs. Ted was whistling softly as he clipped away.

Hands reached out and picked up a bottle. Dark liquid was poured out and rubbed into the greying hair.

McDonald inspected his shaven face. Jack helped him on with a heavy, tatty overcoat. Thomas watched the transformation as he adjusted his starched white cuffs.

The warders were going undercover.

★ ★ ★

Plumes of steam dotted along the horizon as the *Highland Spirit* powered along, disappearing under a bridge and emerging, billowing steam, on the other side.

Sturm was stitching up Skinstad. Another Boer sat watching, fascinated and slightly fearful. Skinstad was gritting his teeth, under a stark light. Sturm was humming to himself as he worked.

★ ★ ★

Laird was leaving his town house. The door opened and the two Boers carried out Laird's luggage. Campbell appeared and skipped down the steps to hail a cab. He was surprisingly nimble for such a giant. The luggage was loaded in.

★ ★ ★

On the busy station concourse, police constables were inspecting passengers' crates waiting for a Liverpool bound train.

One passenger, a portly red-faced man, took exception to the search.

"This is an outrage. An outrage."

The officer was polite, but unmoved.

"Sorry, sir, but we have reason to believe a gang of antiques thieves may be operating in this area."

"What? Preposterous."

The crate causing such concern was wrenched open by two officers using crowbars. They lifted out a large stuffed fox.

The officers looked blankly at each other. The gentleman looked extremely angry as he snatched back his treasure.

★ ★ ★

The *Highland Spirit* slowly drew into Glasgow Central station. Sturm was standing at one of the door windows, taking in the city, dark and faintly menacing. By African standards it had been a short journey. For Sturm, it had been too long. He wanted the ground beneath his feet.

★ ★ ★

Four hundred miles away, at the entrance to Euston station, a cab pulled up at the end of the rank. Janni stepped out, and held the door open for Laird. The lord adjusted his cuffs, as he waited for his luggage to be loaded onto a porter's barrow. His cane twisted in his hand as he stepped out of the cab.

★ ★ ★

Inspector Reeves took another sip of his cold tea. The map of London hung over the edge of the desk. It still occupied him.

The Inspector looked up as Hinchcliffe knocked on the door and entered hurriedly.

"The files you asked for, sir."

Reeves was brisk.

"Tea. Hot tea."

"Sir."

Hinchcliffe closed the door behind him.

The Inspector picked up the top file. It was Argyle's service record. Reeves frowned slightly, as he reached across for another file.

★ ★ ★

A porter pushed his barrow with Laird's luggage piled high on it through the crowded, jostling station. Laird strode along just ahead of it, Campbell towering at his side. Janni and Halle walked a couple of paces behind, flanking Laird.

The *Northern Scot* rested majestically at the platform. As they passed the engine, whistling could be heard. It was *Greensleeves*.

A shorn, bespectacled Battle was standing on the engine plate shovelling coal into the furnace's mouth.

Ron, an oil-stained driver, raised an eyebrow at Battle.

"Bob got the trots again, eh?"

Battle paused. He considered his answer.

"Yeah, poor old Bob, chained to the seat."

In a dark cubicle, Bob, the stoker, was gagged and tied to the toilet seat.

Battle paused slightly to watch Laird's party pass.

The driver glanced at him.

"Looks like a right toff, guv." Battle flicked a thumb at Laird's back.

Ron nodded.

"Regular traveller that. Lord Laird. Some Scottish duke."

Battle wiped the sweat from his eyes, shrugged and started working again.

The guard raised his flag and blew his whistle.

Battle looked up at the shrill sound of the whistle. He peered at two police constables standing on the platform. Head down again, he concentrated on his shovel and the coal.

Chapter Twelve

Steaming North

In the luxury of the first class carriage, Laird was settling in.

Laird chose a seat by the window. Campbell was putting a small case on the overhead netted rack.

Laird nodded his dismissal, but as Campbell moved to obey, the door opened.

The greeting was thrown out; a voice used to being heard.

"Good morning. Would there be room here for one of God's foot soldiers?"

Without waiting for a reply, a priest shuffled in and laid his case on one of the empty seats. He sat back and nodded to an irritated Laird and the towering Campbell.

Above the dog collar, Keilty smiled.

★ ★ ★

Reeves's office lacked air.

The man was suffocating under the pressure of this case.

On his chaotic desk, lay a large white pad with a rough flow diagram of words, dates and lines scrawled on it. The words: 'Tower', 'McDonald', 'Battle', 'Keilty', 'PC Stephen – Thames'.

Inspector Reeves wrote in 'Argyle – Serpentine'. The pen drew a thin line from 'McDonald' to a blank area. Another line followed from 'Argyle' to the same blank place. Slowly he wrote in two words, his pen scratching the paper, 'Lord Laird'.

★ ★ ★

The *Northern Scot* moved off from Euston station. Clouds of steam filled the platform.

Battle looked up from his labour and grinned through his spectacles. This was the kind of jaunt he had joined the army for.

Laird rustled his *Times*. Keilty smiled. Laird looked up to find that the priest had a flat wooden briefcase perched on his knees and was playing *patience* on it. Keilty looked up. He indicated the cards.

"It's a virtue. Patience, that is."

Keilty the priest smiled. Laird turned his attention back to his newspaper. *Infernal missionaries.*

* * *

Glasgow Central station was filled with cheerful chaos, as Sturm stepped down from the last of the *Highland Spirit's* passenger carriages. Behind him stood two goods wagons. Sturm raised his hand to Kruger, who was already on the platform, half way along the train.

Passengers were still climbing down, being greeted by relatives; hugs and kisses, shouts echoing down the platform. Kruger stood, cupping a match to his cigarette. He watched as some of his men walked past.

Skinstad climbed down gingerly, aided by a colleague, his head and jaw bandaged.

Kruger looked back towards the rear of the train to where Sturm had been minutes before.

Sturm was no longer there. Neither was the end of the train. The freight wagons had vanished.

* * *

Janni and Halle were sitting in the second class carriage on the *Northern Scot*. Campbell made his way along the carriage. Campbell leaned in.

"Check the train."

The Boers showed a flash of resentment, but obeyed. Janni and Halle viewed Campbell with wary dislike and a healthy dose of fear. They had quietly agreed earlier that if any man could take on Otto Sturm, it was the giant sikh.

Halle moved through the train. He scanned the passengers as he walked, while the *Northern Scot* whistled along. His gait was unsteady; he had yet to master the roll of the locomotive. A gifted horseman in his own land, he preferred being in the saddle.

★ ★ ★

Parked outside Laird's London residence was a dark police car. Inspector Reeves, Sergeant Tucker and Constable Hinchcliffe were standing on the steps to the imposing townhouse. The constable rang the doorbell repeatedly, but there was no answer. Reeves impatiently looked at his watch.

"Get around the back, Hinchcliffe, see if there's a servants' entrance. Hop to it." Reeves's exasperation showed.

★ ★ ★

Keilty the priest was tutting to himself as he played his card game. Laird looked annoyed, yet his good manners prevailed. Keilty studied his cards and he picked out the jack of diamonds as his third card. He considered it and looked across at Laird. His smile was just a little crooked as he laid the card down.

★ ★ ★

Glasgow Central was teeming. Porters rushed to aid

passengers with their luggage. Stacks of leather bound trunks were being hauled onto sturdy wooden barrows.

Skinstad was with Rudi, a squat bearded man, helping him walk off the platform, and negotiating the crammed hall.

A woman noticed the wounded Skinstad.

"Sore head, man?" Her hand on her hip.

Skinstad stared at her. He looked hostile. Rudi smiled.

"Dental surgery," he explained.

"That's why I dinnae bother."

The woman smiled with a very bad, uneven set of teeth. The Boers moved on.

★ ★ ★

Halle reached the end of the *Northern Scot* entering the final carriage from the passageway. A guard was sitting smoking in the mail carriage. The guard nodded to Halle. The Boer looked into a partitioned area, where a scruffy looking McDonald was snoring on some mail sacks, a near empty bottle at his feet. Halle frowned.

The guard laughed.

"Ratted, mate. Absolutely kalied. Just letting him sleep it off."

Halle looked dismissive.

In the cushioned first class, the card game continued.

"Damn! Forgive me, Father."

Keilty beamed at Laird. The peer returned to his paper.

After a few seconds, Laird put down his paper and stood up. He pulled out his pocket watch and stretched.

"If you'll excuse me, Father. Lunch."

Laird edged out of the carriage, drawing the door closed behind him.

Keilty nodded to himself.

"*Bon Appetit*, you old devil."

Laird eased into his seat in the dining carriage. He pulled out his napkin. He looked out of the window as the hills rolled by and smiled to himself. *Not long now*.

"Would you like to look at the wine list, sir?" The waiter's voice intruded.

Laird was pulled back from his thoughts.

"Yes."

He took the list. Made a quick decision.

"The claret, '96."

Thomas, in a waiter's black and white, took the wine list back from him.

"Thank you, sir. Fine choice."

Laird glanced at him, as Thomas, the wine waiter, shuffled away.

The engine was hot.

Battle was standing looking down the track. He wiped his face. The driver clapped him on the back and offered him a tin cup. Battle toasted him and the engineer, who was sitting sipping his drink.

Careful not to spill a drop of the claret, Thomas poured the dark red wine into Laird's glass.

★ ★ ★

Kruger stood looking across the River Clyde. He turned. Behind him, Sturm was organising the lifting of crates onto a boat. Sturm shouted instructions. Cargoes were being loaded aboard much larger vessels. Ships bound for the Americas; transatlantic freighters heading for Boston and Nova Scotia. Kruger admired the Americans; they had fought and beaten the British.

Kruger turned back and scanned the boat. Standing on the deck was Skinstad. His face still bandaged. He stared back. Kruger smiled cruelly.

A crate was lowered onto the deck of the boat. Sturm was directing operations. He looked beyond the crate at Skinstad. The bandaged face showed no reaction.

★ ★ ★

Thomas was polishing glasses in a pristine kitchen. Intermittently, he glanced into the dining carriage where Laird was still enjoying his luncheon.

★ ★ ★

Laird's cook was sitting sweating in front of Reeves and Tucker. The cook looked scared, like a rabbit between two stoats. In the dimly lit cell, the only light fell on the frightened woman, while the policemen circled in the shadows.

★ ★ ★

Laird was asleep, gently rocked by the motion of the train. Keilty was still playing cards, his eyes alternating between the cards and the sleeping peer.

Further down the rolling train, Campbell and Halle were dozing. Janni stretched his shoulders; he needed movement, the train felt like an elongated cage. He walked down the carriage, a slim man, light on his feet.

Battle was covered in sweat, his muscles bulging as he shovelled the coal into the furnace.

"Blow this for a game of soldiers."

Halle woke up as the train rocked and jolted heavily. Facing him was an empty seat. Janni was not there. Halle frowned.

He looked across at the lolling Campbell. Halle rose and looked down the carriage. He stood and walked in the opposite direction to the one that Janni had gone.

Halle tried to walk with the rolling motion of the train. He scanned the faces. No sign of Janni.

As Halle came into the mailroom, he scanned the room. There was no guard. McDonald the drunk was no longer there. Wind from an open sliding door tugged at Halle. He moved towards the gaping door.

The *Northern Scot* shot onto a viaduct.

Halle cautiously edged to the open door and peered out. As he jerked back from the opening, linked hands clubbed him in the back.

Halle fell from the train, as it crossed the viaduct, his body plummeting to the ground.

Mac watched him fall.

"Welcome to Scotland, laddie."

Mac pulled the sliding door closed.

Janni made his way back towards his seat. Campbell was still sleeping. Halle was not there. Janni looked down the carriage and settled back into his seat. Janni closed his eyes.

★ ★ ★

A small boat left the Glasgow quayside. At the helm was Sturm. Kruger stood at the doorway. He watched the boat manoeuvre away from land. He turned to find Skinstad staring at his back. Kruger stared back and his subordinate lowered his eyes and moved behind the wheelhouse. Kruger looked satisfied. He could sense Skinstad's hate and his fear; it was right to fear the leader of the pride.

★ ★ ★

The *Northern Scot* hurtled along.

Janni moved with purpose along the aisle, looking for Halle.

He stopped where Campbell was still sleeping. He reached over and roughly shook him. Campbell jolted to wakefulness.

"What…"

Janni leaned in.

"Halle is missing."

Campbell was conscious of the other passengers.

"Quiet. You'll wake the entire train."

Campbell rose. He leaned in close, towering over the young Boer.

"Come with me."

Laird's eyes were closed, so too were the priest's, when there was a gentle knock at the door.

Campbell slid the door open. Janni was with him.

"Excuse me, Sahib, we may have a slight problem."

He looked at his master and then at the sleeping priest.

Laird dismissed Campbell's caution.

"He's gone to the wind. What is it?"

Janni answered him.

"Halle has disappeared."

"Have you searched the train?"

"Yes."

"Well, he can't have got off. Search again. Properly this time and report back to me."

Janni hesitated.

Laird's voice was a hiss.

"Get on with it, man. You, too, Campbell."

The door slid closed behind them.

Laird caressed his cane and took a kerchief out to mop his brow. Keilty dozed. Laird turned to study his own reflection in the glass as the hills flashed past. Keilty's face was hidden from Laird; one eye opened and the Irishman smiled momentarily.

Campbell moved down the aisle.
　Janni was moving away through a carriage.
　Campbell pushed open the dining car doors.
　"Can I help you, sir?"
　Campbell looked up at the voice. Thomas was apologetic, interrupted as he was resetting the dining tables.
　"The dining car closed half an hour ago, sir. Was there something you were after?"
　Campbell pointed past Thomas.
　"What's through there?"
　Thomas followed Campbell's finger with a shrug of the shoulders.
　"Through there, sir? Why just the kitchen and the engine. We wouldn't get very far without it."
　Campbell looked unmoved.
　"No one's been through here?"
　Thomas looked perplexed.
　"I'm looking for a friend," said Campbell.
　"Well, you won't find any friends through there, sir."
　Campbell frowned slightly at Thomas's undertone.

Janni stepped over the sacks in the mailroom. The guard looked up, he had drifted off to sleep. Janni was about to speak.
　McDonald stirred, his voice a slur.
　"What you having? I'll buy yer a drink."
　Janni looked at the drunken man sprawled on the mail sacks.
　"Pay no attention to 'im. He's worse for the drink," said the guard.

Janni studied the drunk's grubby face and turned to the guard.

"Is this the last carriage?"

The guard nodded. Janni angrily turned away.

McDonald started to put the bottle to his lips, but did not take in any liquor, his eyes watchful.

Chapter Thirteen

Glasgow Supper

The tug was riding the waves towards a small island. Drumgoyne rose out of the dark sea. Rugged, unwelcoming cliff faces touched the brooding clouds above it. The cliffs formed a ring around the island, except for a couple of small desolate coves. They fell away to form the harbour shaped almost like a cup cut out of the rock. Kruger had studied the maps and knew every contour. He watched as a couple of Afrikaners were sick over the side. The tug lurched, pushed upwards and sideways by the swelling undercurrents as the boat turned towards Drumgoyne. Kruger watched them grim-faced. Not for the first time, he missed the heat and harshness of his homeland.

★ ★ ★

The *Northern Scot* was stationary in Carlisle Citadel station. Janni climbed down from one of the carriages. He moved along the platform staring in at the train. A few yards behind him, Campbell was doing the same inside the train. Janni looked tense and worried.

The station guard raised his flag and blew his whistle. Janni looked up and down the platform. The train started to move. He stepped nimbly aboard.

Outside the first class carriage, Laird was standing with Janni and Campbell.

Laird's voice was low and urgent:

"There's no need to panic. We can't stop the train without causing a commotion and THAT we cannot afford."

Janni stared at the lord with contempt.

Laird's voice bored into Janni.

"Kruger put you at my command. Any failings will be reported to him. Am I making myself clear?

"Your man may merely have fallen asleep somewhere. It's just a couple of hours to Glasgow. Keep looking."

Janni remained silent and unhappy.

Laird marched to his carriage and pulled open the door to find the priest was asleep.

"Get me a coffee, Campbell, and be quick about it."

★ ★ ★

In Drumgoyne Harbour, the tug was tied up. The crates were being lifted onto the jetty. Kruger stood in the shadows smoking quietly. He looked up at the small row of stone houses along the shore. Sturm was organising the lifting. Commandeered barrows were being used to transport the crates to a horse and cart.

Kruger moved towards the cart. Two disgruntled islanders, Ritchie and MacLeod, stood watching the work. One of the Boers pointed them in Kruger's direction.

Kruger watched their approach, like a waiting cat, assessing their weaknesses.

Ritchie, the older of the two men, doffed his cap, but his voice was impatient.

"Will you be long with the cart? It'll be needed at dusk up the hill."

Kruger looked up, meeting his gaze with his scarred face.

"You'll get it back when we are finished."

Ritchie looked about to speak again.

"When we've finished."

The highlanders looked unhappy, but not unhappy enough to challenge the scarred man.

★ ★ ★

The *Northern Scot* was curving into the outskirts of Glasgow.

Battle was looking at the cityscape as the locomotive began the steady run into Glasgow Central station.

Along the train, passengers were standing reaching for their luggage.

Laird watched the station come closer. In the glass, he noticed the priest looking at him. He turned and returned the stare.

Keilty smiled benignly.

"A fine day to welcome us to a fair city."

Laird continued to study the priest.

"Good day, Father."

★ ★ ★

The heavily loaded cart edged its way up the narrow road, through the centre of Drumgoyne, Rudi and another Boer on the cart, two more trudging alongside.

The cart laboured between the grand front gates, waved on by an Afrikaner acting as guard. The cart continued its journey towards the house, where Kruger was waiting for it.

He signalled and three other men stepped forward to help unload the crate. Rudi jumped down.

"That's the last of it. My God, this is some place."

Kruger's dissatisfaction was evident.

"Where's Sturm?"

"Said he'd stay onboard and set the boat ready for the rendezvous."

Kruger nodded.

"The village?"

Rudi was still looking in awe at the castle.

"Quiet. I left Pieter and Franze to keep it that way. Alright if I have a look around?"

"After you're done sightseeing, check the perimeter guards." Kruger turned away. He had not come to Scotland to sightsee.

★ ★ ★

Glasgow Central station was a picture of controlled mayhem. Campbell was directing some porters to push Laird's luggage. Laird, in a cape and hat, was waiting for Janni. He was growing impatient.

Janni stepped down from the train. As he walked along the platform, he passed Thomas, now in civvies climbing down. Thomas watched him.

Laird tapped his cane impatiently.

Janni stopped in front of Laird.

"No sign."

Laird's attention was caught by a commotion at the far end of the platform, towards the rear of the train. Two police constables were talking to the train's guard. One of the police officers stepped onboard.

Laird turned back to Janni.

"I said what now?" Janni's tone was uneven.

The police officer was helping a drunk down onto the platform. The drunk was bent over, clutching his stomach.

"Now we leave." Laird looked further down the platform.

Another man approached the constables and their charge. He talked quietly to the officers and reluctantly they nodded. He took the drunk's arm and led him across the platform. It was the priest.

Laird frowned slightly. The constables were walking this way.

Laird turned sharply and marched towards the station exit. Janni kept his anger in check.

Two pairs of eyes, Thomas's and Battle's, watched them go. They made eye contact. Battle hopped down from the engine, pulling on his jacket and followed Laird's party.

Thomas turned the other way.

In the station washroom, McDonald was washing his face. Keilty had removed the dog collar. Thomas entered. From a small suitcase, he pulled a new collar and tie for McDonald.

"Where have…?"

Thomas did not let him finish.

"Tommy's dealing with it."

Thomas turned to Keilty.

"Where's the trunk?"

"On the platform."

Thomas nodded.

McDonald was not satisfied.

"If Tommy loses them."

"He won't," said the Welshman, "either they've gone directly to the docks or Laird's planning an overnight stay. My guess is that he's bolting for his hole."

McDonald looked at him before turning to study his reflection.

"We need a boat, Mac."

McDonald sighed.

"I ken."

McDonald straightened up.

"Time to meet the Clyde-side pirates."

★ ★ ★

Drumgoyne's Great Hall was stacked with crates. Perched on one of them in a dark recess was Skinstad. He was rhythmically stropping with an ugly curved knife.

Long, dark, wooden beams met at the apex of the Great Hall's roof. It was majestic, watched over by the heads of fallen stags spaced along its panelled walls.

Kruger entered the hall. Kruger looked at Skinstad and the blade. Kruger turned to give some instructions, before turning back to look at the mass of crates. Skinstad had frozen. His eyes followed Kruger.

★ ★ ★

Thomas, McDonald and Keilty walked across the station foyer, with the trunk and the Irishman's case balanced on a barrow. They were met by Battle.

"The docks," said Battle, confirming Thomas's theory.

Thomas nodded. McDonald scowled slightly.

Thomas beamed at his colleagues.

"One small task before we venture forth. I'll meet you there. Beef for me."

The others watched him.

"What the blinkin' hell…" Battle was flustered.

Keilty patted him on the back.

"Have faith, Tommy."

Battle looked at McDonald. The big highlander relaxed and smiled.

"Aye. I am rather peckish."

Battle nodded his agreement.

In the station café, the four sat sipping mugs of tea, empty supper plates on the table. Condensation coated the café's windows, forming a damp curtain of privacy for the four men.

Thomas beamed wryly at them.

"An army marches on its stomach."

"I sleep on mine," answered Battle, "So what now?"

Thomas inclined his head to McDonald.

"It's your show now, Mac."

McDonald's smile was ruthless.

Thomas was standing on the quayside on a rise above the moored boats. He was studying a vessel, the *Pauline*, through small binoculars. She was a small boat, a blend of rust and faded pale blue paint, suited to short-term hauls and coarse weather; toughened to the biting wind and unpredictable currents.

"Will she do, Mac?"

McDonald's face was fierce and ready.

"Aye, she'll do very nicely."

The *Pauline's* skipper, a tough, tattooed man, leaned out of the wheelhouse, wiping his hands with an oily rag. His young deckhand, Archie, was squatting with a cigarette.

The skipper aimed a kick at him.

"Who told you to stop? Get me a brew." Part of Archie's job was to keep his rough tongued Glaswegian skipper supplied with hot tea – the harsher the better.

The deckhand began to move, but was distracted.

A man was walking along the quayside. The skipper followed the crewman's stare. The stranger gave a slight wave and jumped aboard. The skipper frowned and planted his feet firmly. The deckhand rose to his feet. Something in the gait of the newcomer urged caution.

The man was McDonald. He stopped four or five feet from the seamen.

"Morning. Fine looking vessel. Is she for hire?"

The skipper inclined his head slightly.

"That depends."

McDonald smiled quizzically.

The skipper gave a crooked smile.

"On the price, the job and who's paying."

McDonald nodded as if an agreement has been made.

"That's fine then, laddie. Prepare to cast off."

The skipper tensed.

"I don't think you followed me there, Big Man. I'll be needing more than a few words from some fine speaking teuchter."

McDonald smiled again despite the intended insult. 'Teuchter' meant country yokel to the Glaswegian, but McDonald was proud to be a highlander. Now, he had the skipper's measure.

"Would this be what you're after?"

His palm opened revealing the doubloon. Like lightning, he spun it in the air. The skipper reached out to catch it, as McDonald hit him in the chest. McDonald chopped across Archie's neck and the deckhand went down gurgling. The skipper was struggling to catch his breath, the coin forgotten. He could see two more men climbing aboard with a trunk between them. He turned slightly and became aware of another presence. Through the skipper's pained vision, Battle stood two feet beyond him.

Battle shook his head ruefully.

"Sloppy footwork, Mac. Always use your feet."

Battle's magnified fist crashed in to the skipper. The deck came up to meet the Glaswegian.

McDonald stepped forward and gracefully picked up the doubloon.

"We can't all be artists, Tommy."

Keilty and Thomas, struggling with the trunk, heard the exchange.

"We all know what kind of artist, too, more's the pity," laughed Keilty.

Thomas was slightly breathless.
"Get them below and this thing."
He used his toe against the trunk.

★ ★ ★

A carriage carrying Laird, Janni and Campbell passed through the Drumgoyne Estate gates and approached the castle.

Chapter Fourteen

"Remember Me?"

The *Pauline* left her moorings quietly. Keilty moved nimbly to throw the final tie-rope onboard from the quayside and leapt across the gap as the vessel moved off.

Keilty appeared at the door of the wheelhouse. McDonald was at the helm. Behind him, perched on a shallow bench-seat, Thomas was sitting by an open trunk. He fished out an Enfield rifle. Thomas's eyes moved from the rifle to Keilty and Mac.

"To work, gentlemen." Thomas patted the weapon.

Keilty's smile was thin and cold.

★ ★ ★

The Commissioner was pouring tea from a beautiful china pot. He sighed as he put down the strainer.

There was a knock at the door.

"Come in!"

Another knock at the door.

"COME IN FOR HEAVEN'S SAKE!"

The door opened and a worried looking Constable poked his head in.

The constable stood to attention.

"Derwent, sir. 639D, sir. From the telegram room, sir."

The Commissioner stared at him. Derwent swallowed and tried again.

"This came in, sir. For you, sir. Reads like a puzzle, sir."

"Well, read it, man."

Derwent stuttered.

"Jewels and four missing ravens flying north. Glengoyne Estate, Isle of Drumgoyne. RSM EHT."

The Commissioner's tea was upended as he snatched the message.

He scanned it rapidly, eyes racing over the two sparse lines.

"You. Get me Inspector Reeves. Tell him to meet me at Euston."

★ ★ ★

Laird strode into the Great Hall. He was transfixed. Kruger, Janni and Campbell trailed him.

The room was enormous, the walls panelled with dark mahogany. Stags' heads dominated the panels, staring into the hall, the windows high and curving to form pointed stone arches. Swords, sabres and claymores, and ageing muskets aligned on one wall. The furniture matched the walls: dark, old and heavy. It was a room out of time, with a great fire hearth, a room for feasts to celebrate the bringing down of the stag.

The only colour was provided by the twisted curtains and the pale faces in the gilt framed pictures that were interspersed with the stags' heads. The stone floor was overlaid with Afghan rugs.

Laird spun on his heels. Portraits of his ancestors stared down on him. He pointed to a crate.

"Campbell."

Campbell moved to open it.

Kruger moved forward slightly.

"Is that wise?"

Laird turned, his eyes blazing.

"Indulge an old man."

Kruger stiffened.

"You still haven't sufficiently explained what happened to Halle. And what of McDonald?" asked Kruger.

Laird was dismissive.

"Sufficiently? My WILL is sufficient. My will has brought us here, Amon Kruger."

Laird held up a finger.

"Halle probably got knifed following a skirt. McDonald? Who is he? A squaddie elevated beyond his station by a small dark twist of fate. My will has brought us here and I will see my treasure. Carry on, Campbell."

Laird turned his back on the Afrikaners. Kruger stared at the greying head.

"Very well, M'lord, but the rendezvous is set for tomorrow morning."

But Laird was not listening.

"Leave me to taste my triumph."

★ ★ ★

The *Pauline* was approaching the dark outline of the island of Drumgoyne.

McDonald was manning the helm. Keilty was checking the weapons, while Thomas was at the door surveying the island.

Battle's head appeared at floor level at the top of the ladder that led into the hull, at the back of the wheelhouse deck.

McDonald turned the wheel.

"We have to approach from the north east. Ged and I will go ashore there and make our way overland. If I'm right, he'll have stored the jewels at the castle."

Battle checked he had heard correctly.

"Castle? Who said anything about storming a ruddy castle?"

McDonald was not be deflected.

"Evan, you and Tommy take the boat around south east and aim to hit the village at 1100 hours. That should give us enough time to get into position."

McDonald looked across at Evan, who was still gazing at the island.

"It's beautiful, Mac. Whatever made you leave it?"

He turned back to his view. McDonald stared at the Welshman as if he had just uttered a prophecy. *Mac was seeing the jagged cliffs of Drumgoyne on the day he had left the island to join the Gordon Highlanders.*

"What do we do when we reach the village?" asked Battle.

McDonald pulled himself back to the plan.

McDonald took the direct approach.

"You ram the pier. Then head up the road. The estate is just under a mile away."

★ ★ ★

Drumgoyne village was quiet. Fishermen were mending nets. From his up-turned barrel, Ritchie looked across at a Boer sitting in one of the fishing vessels. The harbour porter, Ritchie, carted goods up to the castle. The newcomers had taken his barrow, now he had to heave everything by hand.

Another Boer was sitting on the deck of the tug. Ritchie looked up the jetty.

A handsome, raven-haired woman was carrying a wicker basket along the shore street. Her name was Karen Gordon. She was not a young woman, but you don't have to be young to be beautiful. The fishermen greeted her as she passed, Ritchie giving her a wave.

Ritchie was not the only man watching her. Watching the

woman, his face half covered by the shadow of the doorway, was Skinstad. Only his good side showed. As the woman approached, he smiled. She stared at him with bright inquisitive eyes, smiling slightly back she walked on.

★ ★ ★

The Commissioner was giving orders as he climbed into a police car. Officers were running to obey. The courtyard at New Scotland Yard was in a frenzy. The Commissioner's face was a shiny red. His blood was up. Derwent came scurrying out of the building.

"You. Derwent. Where's Reeves?"

"Scotland, sir. He left this morning, sir. Is he after the ravens, sir?"

"Get in!"

The Commissioner banged the car's roof

"Euston station and hurry."

The car screeched forwards and skidded into the street, scattering pigeons and pedestrians.

★ ★ ★

Inspector Reeves and Sergeant Tucker watched the countryside whiz past, a young constable dozing beside them.

Tucker broke the silence.

"Have you been to Scotland before, sir? They say it's beautiful."

Reeves looked tired and gave his subordinate a sour look. Tucker, who had never ventured out of London before, turned back to the fast moving countryside.

★ ★ ★

In the castle shadows, Skinstad watched Campbell and two of his countrymen prising open crates.

Laird skipped from one box to another.

"It must be here somewhere. Keep looking."

Skinstad finished stropping his with blade and tucked it away. His stomach was growling and he knew where to find food.

Skinstad emerged from the castle's front entrance. Rudi and another Boer eyed him cautiously. Skinstad's smile was discouraging, but he only showed his good side. It was a habit he was developing.

★ ★ ★

Battle was purring over the *Pauline's* engine.

"You lovely old girl."

He turned to address two prone figures sweating on the engine room floor.

"Nice old lady you got here."

Archie and the skipper had their hands tied and mouths gagged. Archie looked terrified, a mouse staring at a cat. The skipper looked hurt, angry and mean.

Battle considered him. The skipper averted his eyes.

"Tut, tut. Wrong again, me old son. We ain't the villains, we're the flamin' cavalry."

Battle laughed at his own humour.

"Never mind. Soon be done to rights."

The *Pauline* was manoeuvred off a small cove. A thin line of sand provided a break in the scarred overhanging cliffs. Thomas was at the wheel. Battle, his shoulders bulging, lowered a small rowing boat, with McDonald and Keilty aboard. McDonald gave the thumbs up sign and Battle released the winch.

McDonald wheeled the small rowing boat away from the

Pauline. He pulled hard to swing the boat, which doubled as the *Pauline's* lifeboat, around.

"I was born here, Ged."

Keilty with his small wooden case on his knees, nodded back calmly. His face had no expression, except perhaps a mild inquisitiveness.

The rowing boat headed towards the narrow beach under the cliffs. It ducked and bobbed, as McDonald struggled against the current. The sea and the cliffs were black slabs. McDonald aimed for the beach. He was not looking forward to the climb, but Keilty sat upright, relaxed, like a missionary heading to church.

Hanging on by his boot tips, McDonald looked up from his climb. Sweat blanketed his face. The exertion was telling.

Keilty looked down at his comrade. Keilty had reached the top. He hammered a spike into the ground, looped a rope around his waist and lay flat on the ground.

McDonald struggled on. His face hardened. Another couple of feet. He reached up to grip one of the pegs Keilty had left. McDonald stretched again. His face torn with effort, as his hand missed the peg. He slipped.

His cry was cut off by the vice-like grip of Keilty's hand on his wrist. McDonald looked up into the cold blank eyes of the Irishman.

Mac had not fought all over the globe to die on Drumgoyne.

McDonald's will swelled. His toe found purchase. He swung his other hand up and hauled himself to the final peg.

McDonald appeared at the top of the cliff. He rolled away from the edge. He was breathing heavily.

Keilty was lighting a cigarette. For him, the ascent had been an elementary one. A year ago, he had been a member of the ill-fated expedition to conquer Mount Everest, which had claimed the lives of two of his fellow mountaineers, Mallory and Irvine.

Keilty began to pack away his rope, an Enfield slung over his back.

Keilty looked to the Scot. McDonald nodded and hauled himself to his feet. Keilty picked up his wooden briefcase and the two turned inland.

Sturm was sitting on the deck of the tug, his sleeves rolled up.

Along the shore, a lone figure was walking towards the tug. Sturm recognised Ritchie. The persistent Islander was becoming a nuisance.

The narrow track ran down towards a small croft, a single storey granite stone house. A small dwelling huddled against the hillside. Washing was flapping furiously in the blustering wind.

Skinstad was following Karen, as she disappeared behind some of the washing. He had seen her buy bread and fruit at the village.

When he reached the croft, there was no sign of anyone. Only the rows of sheets and shirts billowing like giant flags.

Skinstad rapped on the door. His smile froze as the door opened. Two barrels of a shotgun were inches from his face.

Skinstad's smile widened to cover his shock, but that only served to make him appear more grotesque as his face swelled under Sturm's tight stitches.

"This is my hoose and ye'll leave now." The gun was steady in Karen's hand.

Skinstad nodded slowly.

This was no time to be rash. The Afrikaner edged backwards as Karen advanced. He kept his hands in full view.

Skinstad pushed the flapping washing aside as he carefully retreated.

The Afrikaner lurched to the side as a body crashed into

him. Skinstad fought back. A forehead smashed into his nose. McDonald breathed down on him.

"Remember me?" Mac's words were through clenched teeth.

Recognition came to the Boer. He smashed his fist into the side of McDonald's head. Again a blow like a bludgeon. The third blow sent McDonald reeling.

Skinstad leapt up. He moved to rush McDonald as the old soldier began to stand. Skinstad stopped. Blood covered his lower face. Keilty stood at the corner of the croft.

Karen was bewildered by the sudden combat in front of her. She strode forward aiming her gun. It was knocked upwards, discharging the shot into the air.

Robert Gordon, Karen's brother, was chopping logs at the rear of the croft. His swinging action froze as the shotgun blast and Karen's scream seared through the air. He leapt over the splintered woodpile and charged around the cottage with the axe swinging in his hand.

Robert Gordon leaped over the dyke and took in the sight of his sister and the three men. The third man was Keilty, holding Karen's gun as though it is a walking stick.

Skinstad's grin became more malevolent.

McDonald pointed at him.

"Just you and me."

Skinstad laughed. It broke the spell and Gordon rushed at him with his axe. Keilty's leg upended him. Keilty placed his boot on the ghillie's spine.

"It's their fight."

Gordon strained to see his sister. She was regaining her composure. She nodded to her brother, reassuring him that Keilty meant her no harm.

Skinstad laughed again and moved in a half circle. McDonald took a deep breath and edged the other way. Skinstad slid forward.

"You're a dead man, Engelsman."

With cat-like speed, Skinstad leapt forward, slashing with his knife. Karen and Gordon flinched at the appearance of the weapon.

The blade flashed across McDonald's arm, severing McDonald's coat. Unlike their last meeting, this time, McDonald stepped inside, slamming his elbow and forearm into Skinstad's neck. The Boer's head snapped back as McDonald flicked his fist into Skinstad's shattered nose.

The Afrikaner stepped back to keep his balance. McDonald's other fist pulverised his face. Skinstad swayed. McDonald's boot sent him to his knees. The knife fell to the ground.

Skinstad was on his knees. He tried to clear his head. His hand reached out and his fingers closed on the knife. He pulled himself to his feet. McDonald stood three feet away. The highlander's eyes were brutal.

Skinstad hauled himself to his feet, tightened his grip on the knife and charged. A white shirt flapped across his chest and face. It blew away again, but the shirt remained fastened to Skinstad's chest by a small stabbing knife. McDonald stepped back. Blood seeped onto the shirt. Skinstad's eyes glazed. As he fell the shirt came away from the washing line. It partially covered his inert body.

McDonald looked from Skinstad to the watching trio. Keilty's face registered nothing, the islanders looked bewildered and frightened. McDonald smiled at them.

"I am John Cameron McDonald. This island was once my home."

Chapter Fifteen

Bareknuckled Battle

Kruger was standing with Janni at the main entrance to Drumgoyne Castle.

"The rendezvous is fixed. Sturm said he would stay down with the tug. He said that the natives were getting restless," said Janni.

Kruger nodded.

"Start packing it away. If Laird insists on wearing the crown, indulge him. And watch his man Campbell."

Janni nodded and turned away to obey.

In the sparse, rough-hewed croft, Gordon and Karen were listening to McDonald. It was a small room, with a low ceiling, and McDonald was too tall for the room. Karen sat in an elegant rocking chair. It was the grandest piece of furniture in the house. There was a pitted table for eating and a small stove. Two small windows provided the light. A worn patterned rug on the earthen floor. Mac's energy dominated the room.

"I know Laird is your master. He was mine once."

Gordon acknowledged the point.

"I remember your father. And you, though you left us young, John Cameron McDonald."

McDonald looked surprised and vaguely uneasy.

"You saved Karen's life. Her husband was a cousin of yours."

McDonald looked with a fresh eye at Karen. She met his gaze. Beautiful and wild.

"Your father was a proud man. I'll bide and fight aside you."

Karen stepped forward.

"So will I."

Mac looked put out and about to protest.

"I let one man go away and fight alone. He never came back," said Karen as she looked defiantly at Mac, who was reassessing this woman.

"The Somme."

McDonald nodded. He had fought there, too, but had survived.

"*Bydand*."

"*Bydand*," the motto of the Gordon Highlanders echoed in the small croft.

The two clasped hands. Karen thrust out her hand. Mac nodded slowly and took it.

"*Bydand*," she said.

There came two knocks on the door, followed by two more, and it opened to reveal Keilty.

"Time's short, Mac."

The *Pauline* was just off the headland. Battle and Thomas hauled out the trunk they had brought from London.

Battle settled it down, taking most of the strain.

"Still heavy even without the Enfields."

They set it down near the prow of the boat. Thomas opened it.

Battle was stunned.

"Blinkin' shoot me."

"Hush, Tommy, else you'll tempt fate." Thomas made a sign to ward off evil.

Battle lifted out a Vickers 303-inch machine gun. Thomas hauled out the tripod.

"Where the ruddy hell did you get this from, Doubtin'?"

Thomas gave Battle a wry smile.

"You have some very resourceful relatives, Tommy."

Battle shook his head in wonder, hugging the powerful machine gun.

"Jack's a flamin' marvel."

The light from the croft window fell on the rough wooden table. Keilty's face was serene. In his hands was the sniper's rifle. He pulled out a long gleaming bullet and slotted it into the breech.

At that second, the door opened, Keilty looked up, swinging the rifle in one movement.

Karen looked startled.

"Sorry, I couldn't mind the code."

Keilty smiled. Karen smiled back cautiously. The Irishman meant her no harm, but she sensed how deadly he was. Keilty rose and hoisted the sniper's tool over his head.

Outside, Mac, Keilty and Gordon picked up their guns. As they did so, the croft door opened. Karen had tied back her unruly hair. She had changed and was now wearing hunting gear. In her hand was a hunter's rifle. Mac and Keilty exchanged a glance. Karen noticed it.

"My father taught me. Who taught you?"

This time, Mac smiled. This woman was a warrior. Karen pulled on her bonnet.

Four figures, Gordon, McDonald, Keilty and Karen were running across the open ground, spreading out in an arrow formation.

Thomas checked the machine gun. He turned and gave the thumbs up to Battle in the wheelhouse. The Cockney nodded and swung the boat around.

Thomas made the sign of the cross.

"Our Father, who…"

Battle looked out at his colleague and shook his head in wonder.

"You're a rum dabster, Doubtin'."

Battle looked at his watch. It was five minutes to 11.

"Right on schedule."

A young Boer, Pieter, was dozing on the deck of a small yawl, berthed beside the tug. He turned in the direction of the harbour entrance, as the low purr of a distant engine reached him. The faint hum could be heard above the sound of the sea and it was getting closer.

The *Pauline* rounded the headland. Pieter snatched up his rifle and turned towards the tug.

"Sturm! STURM!"

The giant Afrikaner emerged from the tug's wheelhouse. He followed Pieter's pointing arm. Sturm frowned. The approaching vessel was not slowing, instead, it was heading towards the harbour.

In the lea of a small shed, Ritchie watched the course of the boat with growing interest.

Ritchie's excitement grew.

"They're going to ram them. Go on!"

Sturm looked from the vessel to the pier where he could make out Ritchie's excitement. Sturm's puzzlement was rapidly turning to alarm.

"Vegstellings!(Action stations!)" – he yelled.

Two more Boers rushed from inside the tug, but taking in the rapidly approaching boat, they seemed uncertain what to do. Sturm's eyes widened.

Thomas's eyes could be seen behind the machine gun. He depressed the trigger and the Vickers juddered into action.

Bullets crashed into the side of the tug, cutting a path to where the two Boers were crouching. The first was slammed into the side of the wheelhouse. The second jolted backwards. Sturm dived for cover.

Battle turned the *Pauline* slightly.

"Hang on, Doubtin'!"

The *Pauline* crashed into the small fishing boat beside the tug. Wood splintered. Thomas desperately hung on. Battle was braced in the wheelhouse.

Sturm slid a few feet from the impact.

Pieter was thrown off his feet.

Two more Boers charged out from one of the harbour buildings and started running towards the crash.

Pieter struggled to his feet. He rose to find Battle's Enfield trained on him. He experienced a second of fear and panic, before the retort from Battle's gun sent him sprawling, clutching his leg.

Sturm watched it all.

Battle was moving to get off the stricken *Pauline*.

"Come on, Doubtin'."

Thomas had not heard him. He crawled back to the Vickers and righted it. In his sights were two Boers advancing down the pier. One loosened off a shot, which flew over Thomas's head.

Thomas was chanting.

"And he smote them down…"

The death rattle of the gun drowned his words as the two Boers were cut down.

Battle leapt on to the tug. He turned back.

"Doubtin'! You stupid old Welsh goat, get off there!"

Thomas came out of his reverie and signalled that he understood.

Battle returned the thumbs up signal and turned away. Suddenly, Sturm's fist crashed into his face. Battle was knocked backwards into the railing. He looked up at the huge Afrikaner.

Battle's nose was wrecked. *Not for the first time.*

On the pier, one of the Boers was trying to reach his gun.

He was injured, but could see Sturm and Battle facing each other. A boot landed on his hand. He cried out in pain and twisted to look up. Ritchie's cold face stared back.

"You've come to the wrong island, laddie."

Ritchie brought his boot down hard and picked up the gun.

Outside the castle doors, four Boers stood in confusion at the noise of distant gunshots. Janni and Kruger raced out of the castle.

"What's going on?" Kruger, his voice hard.

Venter pointed towards the village.

"Gunshots. From the harbour."

Kruger and Janni exchanged glances.

Kruger turned back to Venter.

"Take two men and check it out. The locals might be getting jumpy. Where's Skinstad? Find him."

Kruger nodded to Janni.

"Speed up the packing and check the guards."

They rushed to obey. Kruger looked agitated, like a ruffled hawk.

Battle rose to face Sturm. He adjusted his balance on the boat deck.

"Six four, 18 stone. Heavyweight."

Battle wiped blood away from his lower face.

"And a southpaw."

Battle edged forwards.

Sturm's bulging shoulders tensed. A huge haymaker was launched. Battle stepped inside and drilled his fists into the taller man's stomach, dancing away he planted a stinging hook onto Sturm's jaw. The Afrikaner recovered his balance, but the blows hurt.

Thomas appeared eight feet behind Battle's shoulder.

Battle edged forward. Sturm looked powerful. He threw

out two heavy punches. Battle skipped in again. This time Sturm's face took a battering. A vicious combination, followed by two stabbing blows to the kidneys. Sturm looked pained and bewildered.

Sturm's eyes looked wild. He went berserk. Battle ducked to avoid the taller man's reach, smashing his fists in again, but Sturm seemed beyond pain and caught Battle on the top of his head. Battle twisted away, but was cuffed by Sturm's other hand.

Battle rocked back against the railings. Sturm, his mouth and nose bloody, blundered on. He grabbed Battle by the throat and squeezed.

Battle's punches rained into Sturm's kidneys and ribs. The big Afrikaner just squeezed tighter. Battle's efforts grew more frantic. Sturm leaned in and Battle, desperation contorting his face, butted him twice in the face.

Battle powered on, using head and hands, as slowly the great Afrikaner's strength gave way.

Sturm slid backwards, his grip failing, as Battle, his face dark, stepped in close to finish his work.

The lumbering Sturm fell to the deck. His face was a pulp.

Battle looked done. He stared across at Thomas and Ritchie, breathing heavily.

At the rear of Drumgoyne Castle, Otto, a small broad shouldered Boer with a goatee beard, was on guard duty. He was too far away to have heard the attack at the harbour, being at the other side of the castle.

Keilty's eyes narrowed down the barrel of his sights. Slowly, gently, his finger caressed the trigger. The weapon kicked back into his shoulder.

Otto's expression fixed, as the air was pumped out of his lungs by the impact of the round. He crumpled.

Keilty scanned the countryside and gave a hand signal.

Karen was at his shoulder. McDonald and Gordon made a break from cover.

Thomas crouched in the shadow of a building. He watched the road up the hill. He turned and signalled. Battle moved forward. Battle stopped. His face was still bloody. He turned back and waved. Ritchie ran towards him, carrying the rifle and ammo he had taken off the young Boer, Pieter.

Krease trotted across the castle lawn to where Mani was standing by a garden wall. Krease was well named. Like Kruger, his face was scarred, and his mouth twisted by an old burn. Mani, by contrast, was younger, handsome with a shock of blond hair that threatened to curl if it were ever permitted to grow.

"There's some trouble down the harbour. Tell Helt and Otto."

Mani nodded. As Krease headed back to the castle, Mani turned and waved at Helt, who acknowledged and tightened his grip on his rifle. Mani stepped into the outer garden, which was designed as a Victorian maze. However, he seemed to know where he was going. He moved with pace. Right and left. At the third turn, he stepped onto McDonald's knife.

The highlander lowered Mani's body to the ground.

Helt was standing at the second entrance to the outer garden. He had seen Mani go in, but edged closer to the wall. He began a scan of the garden. He responded to a slight coughing noise, but was already dead. His face scraped against the granite stone wall as he fell. Keilty stepped out from the maze.

In the Great Hall, the crates were being sealed. Kruger and Janni moved through the hall, Kruger giving instructions.

"As soon as you're done, take up position at the front gate.

"There could be more to those shots than Skinstad's mischief."

Janni nodded, but looked momentarily frightened.

Laird's private chambers were lavish. The huge four-poster bed hung with weighty velvet curtains. The furniture, all dark and expensive, was made to outlast the Empire. The candlesticks and Laird's hairbrush and mirror were silver.

Laird's ageing hands carefully lifted up a magnificent crown. The elegant fingers lovingly caressed the craftwork, that glinted and shone as he raised it.

Laird's expression was that of a small child.

"Fit for a king."

Venter and four other Boers were running down the steep lane from the castle towards the village.

The sound of their feet on the uneven flagstones echoed down the road.

Thomas stepped out from a side passage, his Enfield buckled. Venter screamed a warning. Battle fired from the other side of the wynd, the narrow street that led up from the harbour. The leading Boer's tunic changed colour. Three of the Boers were cut down. Venter dived for cover.

He lay pressed against a cold wall. He reached across to feel his arm. He had been hit. He swore in Afrikaans.

From his position he could see the body of one dead colleague and the twitching boot of another.

Venter made his decision.

"Kruger."

Using his rifle as a crutch, he lifted himself up.

Through the back yard of a village house, a pair of boots moved quickly.

Venter sensed his predicament. He wiped his face and edged along the passageway. Speeding up, he turned left back up the hill.

The boots moved through a gate, trailing Venter.

Venter froze at the noise, then hastened his retreat. He reached another yard and hugging the wall of a house, turned the corner. Ritchie stood, feet apart at the top of a short stone flight of steps. Ritchie and his rifle stared malevolently at Venter.

"NO!"

The butt of Battle's gun knocked Venter out from behind. Battle nodded at Ritchie. The two moved on.

As Kruger and Janni hurried from the Great Hall, they were met by an agitated Krease.

"More shots and I was close enough to tell they are firing Enfields."

Kruger took this in.

"How many men at the gate?"

Kraese answered:

"Six."

Kruger looked to Janni.

"Tell the packers to hurry."

"They're just about done."

Kruger made his call.

"If there's trouble coming, we sit and wait for it."

Kruger spun away to issue more orders.

Chapter Sixteen

Storming the Castle

McDonald surveyed the castle from the garden wall. He leant back and signalled Keilty. McDonald checked Gordon was with him. He pointed to a doorway.

"That still the kitchen?"

Gordon nodded.

McDonald crouched and sprinted towards the door. Gordon followed. Keilty and Karen covered them.

They reached the doorway. McDonald tried the handle. It was locked.

He turned and signalled Keilty. Pulling out his Webley Mk IV revolver, a souvenir from his service in Africa, McDonald shot the lock, leaning back to empty more rounds into the top and bottom of the door, where the bolts and hinges were.

Kruger and three packers froze at the sound of the nearby shots.

Kruger threw a rifle to one of his men.

"The servants' quarters. Now!"

All the three men rushed to obey. Kruger checked his rifle and strode from the room.

On the other side of the kitchen door, McDonald nodded to Gordon. They charged the door. It gave slightly. A second charge.

Gordon and McDonald burst through the door. The door was still on its hinges and Gordon had been gashed above his left eye by evil looking splinters.

They moved through the large kitchen.

McDonald scanned the room.

"Just how I mind it."

He turned to Gordon.

"I used to deliver game here with my father."

Gordon was binding his hand. That too was seeping blood. Gordon's smile was hard.

"I still do. Where's your Irish friend?"

Mac pointed towards the other side of the castle.

"The others may need some help with the front gate."

McDonald and Gordon moved out of the kitchen into a short dark hallway. A Boer appeared at the far end. He shouted a warning to the other Boers coming down the corridor. Gordon ducked against a doorway, but McDonald dropped onto one knee, moving the rifle up in the same movement to shoot the Boer.

Another appeared, shouted and fired wildly, but McDonald had already turned down a corridor.

Kruger strode towards the open main doors. Three men were stationed at the main entrance. Rifle in his hand, he looked across at the main gates.

"Tell them to keep the gates open. We'll need them tonight."

Keilty was outside, at the corner of the building. From here, he could see the gate clearly and the front entrance by craning his head.

"Any time now."

As if in answer, shots rang out. One of the Boers at the gate fell. Keilty smiled.

Kruger and his men were startled.

"Find out who we're up against," Kruger ordered.

Johannes raced towards the gate, where the exchanges of

fire were coming from.

Keilty shifted his position. Johannes's run halted midway across the lawn. His legs buckled and he fell.

Kruger stared in amazement. He turned to the right to find the source of the shot, amidst the shooting at the gate. The man next to him slammed into the wall. Picked off by the sniper.

Kruger waved his men back.

"Inside!"

At the gatehouse, a handful of Boers were returning fire at a stone dyke. Thomas and Ritchie fired back. The Boers held the better cover. Two of them were shooting from inside a small gatehouse.

Thomas opened his coat and pulled out a flare gun. He slotted in the cartridge.

Thomas caught Ritchie's attention.

"Give me cover."

Ritchie, slightly bewildered, did as he was told. Thomas stood, aimed and fired the flare at the gatehouse. The flare flashed through one of the windows.

"Now!"

Before the two of them had moved a couple of feet, Battle appeared from the other side of the road. Bayonet fixed. He was howling like a Dervish, firing as he ran.

Two Boers scrambled out of the gatehouse. Another fell as Battle emptied his magazine. Thomas and Ritchie followed.

Across the lawn, Keilty dropped one of the Boers emerging from the gatehouse.

The other turned in desperation as Battle charged at him. The Boer raised his rifle, but Battle stepped in knocking the weapon aside with his own and, counting to himself, as if practising a deadly dance ritual, stabbed home the bayonet.

In the entrance hall, Kruger was met by Janni.

He pointed back into the great house.

"They came in through the back. At least two of them. It's the drunk from the train."

"McDonald."

Kruger's scarred face was evil with hate.

"He's mine."

McDonald was moving through the castle. He pushed a door open. It was a bedroom. He scanned the room. Empty. He withdrew. His movements trained, contained, primed.

Keilty rolled away from the building. Now he had a better angle on the main door.

He gave covering fire as Battle, Thomas and Ritchie charged.

Keilty squinted and gently eased back the trigger.

One of the two Boers firing from the archway was hit. The other fired two more wild rounds at the onrushing trio. A loud retort as Karen's bullet took him in the chest. Keilty nodded at her in appreciation of the shot.

Battle, Thomas and Ritchie poured through the entrance and into the hallway. Keilty rose and ran the same way in a crouch. Karen followed, stopping to send another shot at the front door.

Battle charged into Drumgoyne Castle. He stabbed down on the Boer lying on the left and took up position looking into the Great Hall. Thomas crouched at the foot of the wide stairs. Ritchie followed.

The Boer on the right moved slightly. Keilty's shot had not finished him. His gun dragged on the floor. Battle spun around at the noise as the Boer fired. Ritchie was spun off his feet.

Battle levelled his gun, but Keilty's rifle butt beat him to it.

McDonald was moving through the castle corridors. He

stopped as a door ahead of him closed. He paused. McDonald stepped forward very slowly. The doorframe next to him splintered as a bullet slammed into it. McDonald dived for cover.

Kruger stood against a wall at the far end of the corridor.

"Remember Bulwana, McDonald? You shot my father as he rode with Laird. Remember that?"

McDonald listened to place the voice.

"It was our land. Our homeland. We tamed it. Did you think you could steal it?"

"The ravens came home. So will the jewels." McDonald's voice carried down the corridor.

Kruger's cold, twisted laugh floated down the hall like an evil ghost.

Thomas and Keilty were kneeling over Ritchie in the entrance hall. His face was chalk white. Thomas pushed some cloth into the wound.

"Stay awake, man. Sit there and cover the door for us. Can you do that?"

Ritchie, his breath shallow, nodded.

Thomas and Keilty's eyes met. Karen watched the exchange and realised what it meant. There was no hope for Ritchie.

Gordon was advancing slowly and cautiously down a passageway. Like his sister Karen, he was more used to stalking deer high in the glens. This type of room to room fighting was alien to him. He edged forward cautiously. One wrong move could be his last and he knew it.

McDonald was listening, pressed against a doorway. From the end of the long corridor came the merest of movements. Kruger raised his arm and fired.

Kruger waited, then leaned out and loosened another round. Simultaneously, McDonald did the same. They spied each other as the bullets flew wide. Both pressed back in for cover.

The muffled sound of shots reached Battle in the hallway.

"They're upstairs, Ged. Come on, Doubtin'!"

Battle's cry reached Kruger.

Kruger made a decision. He stepped out and fired two shots down the hall, before turning towards the stairs. He moved across the top of the stairs, where Janni was covering them.

As Thomas appeared climbing the sweeping staircase, Kruger leaned out and fired. Janni did the same.

Thomas stumbled backwards, clutching his shoulder.

Battle leapt forwards.

"Doubtin'!"

Kruger signalled Janni and he moved away from the stairs. Kruger followed.

McDonald was pressed into the doorway. From there he heard the shooting near the grand staircase. Slowly he crept forward.

Thomas was slumped on the first landing, when Battle reached him.

"Doubtin', you stupid old duffer."

Thomas grimaced.

"There's two of them. Kruger and the one from the train."

Keilty appeared three steps below. Battle's eyes misted over. He powered up the stairs.

"Cover me, Ged!"

"Tommy!" shouted Keilty in warning.

Battle leaped up the second flight, Keilty in pursuit.

McDonald rounded the corner of the upstairs hallway and saw Janni and Kruger moving away from the stairs. He stepped forward and fired. His shot missed Janni, who fired back. As Battle charged up the stairs, Kruger levelled his pistol.

"You're a dead man, Tommy." Kruger looked down his barrel at Battle and fired.

Battle was propelled backwards.

McDonald, hearing Kruger's words, stepped out and fired again. The Boers retreated.

Keilty reached Battle. The Londoner was struggling for breath.

"He knew my name, Ged." Battle was bewildered.

Keilty looked stricken.

"You're famous, Tommy."

Battle died.

"All the world over." Keilty laid Battle's head back.

"Ged, Tommy! Come up slowly. Watch your right!" Mac shouted from above.

Keilty closed Battle's eyes and lifted his gun.

Keilty climbed cautiously to the top of the stairs. McDonald pointed to where the enemy had gone. Keilty nodded. His face was pitiless.

"Laird's your man, Mac."

McDonald studied his friend's face and accepted his decision.

McDonald watched as Keilty inched forward with catlike stealth. As he did so, Keilty pulled out a pistol and a thin killing knife.

Chapter Seventeen

The Wolf's Bite

McDonald walked slowly down the wide main staircase, pausing to take in Battle's still body. Ritchie was slumped against the ancient stone wall. White-faced and motionless, he gave no sign of life.

McDonald edged into a small hall. He scanned the room and stepped into it. Propped against one of the crates was Gordon. He was wounded, bleeding from a thigh wound.

"He jumped me. Him and his master. He's waiting for you. In the Great Hall."

McDonald examined Gordon's wound. The injured man grimaced.

"I'll live."

McDonald smiled at the man's courage.

"Aye, you will, laddie."

McDonald looked towards the doors that led into the Great Hall.

Tucking away his weapons, Mac picked up Gordon's fallen Enfield, with the bayonet still fixed, and checked the breech. *Old habits keep you alive.*

In the hallway upstairs, Keilty stood at the corner with the stairs behind him. He listened.

At the other end of the wide corridor, Janni and Kruger waited. They looked across at each other.

Keilty stepped across the opening and fired one shot. He reached the other side as two bullets slammed into the wall. One smashed into the doorframe he had been moments before, the other to a foot wide of where he had now moved on to.

He checked his chamber. Five bullets left.

Slowly and carefully, Keilty lowered himself until he was laying full length on the floor. He levelled his sniper rifle and lying down, with one hand, threw it across the opening. Two shots rang out as before. Keilty moved slightly and fired at floor level.

Janni fell backwards clutching his ankle.

Keilty heard the pained Afrikaner swearing. He smiled coldly. He waited.

McDonald stood listening at the double doors that lead into the Great Hall. He turned at a noise. It was Karen. He signalled her to stop. She nodded and offered him a small tight smile.

The giant arched doors burst open, and Campbell, wielding a mighty curved sword charged at McDonald. Karen's mouth formed a warning, but no sound came, as McDonald ducked the blow and swung away. McDonald blocked another heavy stroke with his Enfield. He pushed Campbell back and swung his rifle round, pointing the bayonet at Campbell.

Karen raised her rifle, but the two men were locked together. They were circling too close together for her to get in a clean shot.

Campbell bellowed a war cry and charged again.

This time McDonald stepped forward, deflecting the heavy downward stroke and jabbed the bayonet forward. The men stood, staring at each other.

The bayonet embedded in Campbell's torso. Campbell's sword fell from his hand, ringing as it struck the stone floor. McDonald jerked the bayonet out and Campbell tumbled to the floor.

McDonald studied the body for a second, then turned to face the huge double doors.

"Laird."

Keilty edged down the corridor. He was straining to hear even the smallest of sounds. Nothing. He reached a door and looked down. He was following a trail of blood. It stopped at this door. He looked down the remainder of the corridor, which led into a brighter area, with a huge stained glass window at the end.

He stepped back and kicked the door open and launched himself through it.

Keilty landed and rolled. He came to rest against a giant four-poster bed. He stopped and listened. He slowly scanned the room; the gap between the curtains and the floor, under the bed. His eyes fell on a large wardrobe and a small door on the opposite side of the bed to him.

Keilty frowned. He worked his way along the side of the bed. Blood stains led to the huge wardrobe. He looked at the open door. Raising himself up, he fired twice into the small door. The wardrobe burst open as Janni frantically charged out. Keilty swivelled and loosened two rounds into the wardrobe door and the desperate Afrikaner. Janni crashed back in to the wardrobe's dark recess.

"Did you serve in South Africa?"

Kruger was standing at the door, a pistol aimed at Keilty.

"Herd my mother and sister like cattle into your camps to rot?"

Keilty was still. A knife slid from his cuff.

"You've shot your last bolt, Engelsman."

Keilty's eyes were slits.

"I'm Irish, you ass."

Kruger's scar twitched. Kruger brought up his pistol.

"Is there a difference?"

"Of course, there is. We're Celts." Said Thomas, in a soft burr.

Kruger swung around into the hallway. Thomas, holding his weighty Webley with his good arm, emptied the revolver rounds into Kruger. The kick of the pistol made Thomas's aim wild. Kruger spun against the wall. The bullets turned him in slow motion. The last three sent him smashing through the tall, stained glass window at the end of the corridor.

Thomas lowered the revolver. He was exhausted.

Keilty picked up Kruger's gun, a well-kept Luger, and checked the chamber.

"Let's find Mac, Doubtin'."

McDonald crashed through the double doors into the Great Hall. He landed heavily and covered the room with his rifle. The hall was still packed with crates. There was no sign of Laird.

"A fine entrance. Welcome to my kingdom, McDonald."

McDonald rose to his feet.

"You have always been a thorn, McDonald. I should have left you to die."

McDonald conceded the point.

"Perhaps you should have."

McDonald walked carefully forward; still no sign of Laird.

"But then you'd have had no cover for your treachery."

"Treachery! Who have I betrayed – an uncaring, snobbery-ridden, decaying Empire? Riddled with prejudice and self-loathing. Divide and rule, McDonald. Class and creed, McDonald.

"English despising Scots, laughing at the Irish, pouring scorn on the Welsh.

"Look at me, McDonald, a Lord of the Realm, despised because my mother was a Boer. Look at me!"

McDonald turned to see Laird. The lord was bedecked in full regalia. His manic eyes looked out from under a royal crown, the St. Edward's Crown. It was tilted at an angle as though far too big for him. He was wrapped in a fur cape, which ran to the floor. The lining was rich dark vermillion. Laird's walking cane was in his hand.

"Another mother and I might have risen to the highest office."

McDonald looked at the lord with contempt.

"Another mother and you might have had no title."

Laird fixed McDonald with one eye.

"You were always a little man, McDonald. Do you know what they called me in Africa? Colonel Blood."

"I should have remembered."

"Why? Because I knew how to use the lash."

"That's when it came to me. Colonel Blood. If a Seventeenth Century rogue could pull it off, why not a modern gentleman. And I could watch the Empire crumble."

McDonald planted his feet.

"You're no gentleman."

Laird stopped his tirade to consider the man in front of him.

"Why are you here, Sergeant Major? Do you think you can stop me? The damage has already been done."

"I came to kill you."

Laird looked surprised.

"Kill me? Your own Clan Chief? But we're both Scots, man!"

McDonald snapped.

"You don't even speak my language!"

"No!"

Laird half turned away as if shamed and the crown slipped a little. His hands fiddled with his cane. Unseen by McDonald, he twisted back, drawing a long blade from inside his cane.

"But you'll understand this."

His arm snaked out and Laird lunged forward like a fencer. The blade pierced McDonald's chest. Laird leapt back triumphantly. The handle of the cane, with the wolf's head jutted from McDonald's chest.

"Feel the wolf's bite, McDonald!"

McDonald studied the silver handle. He dropped to his knees. Slowly he raised his arm. The Enfield came up.

Quietly, McDonald mouthed the words,

"*Bydand.*"

Laird's scream filled the Great Hall.

"NO!"

The Enfield went off.

Laird's crown rolled along the floor, coming to rest at McDonald's knees.

The old cemetery was perched on a slant on the Drumgoyne hillside. A Church Minister stood with a small group of mourners. Tight grieving faces. Thomas, Gordon and Karen, Keilty and Inspector Reeves, with a couple of police officers. There was no Battle, McDonald or Ritchie. Thomas had a sling bound around his arm. Gordon, his head and hand bandaged, was supported by Karen. The Minister was speaking, but there was no sound. The wind whipped away his words before they could reach the mourners. Keilty looked at the three graves. He looked across the island; at the beauty of it.

★ ★ ★

General Hastings, Governor of the Tower of London, was at his office window; his customary perch.

"A most disagreeable business. Dreadful shame about Battle and McDonald."

He turned to face Thomas and Keilty.

"Returning to Chelsea, Thomas?"

Thomas considered the question and the Governor.

"Thought I might go and convalesce with some family first, Governor."

The Governor frowned.

"Didn't know you had any."

"Forgotten I had, sir."

The Governor was put out.

"No mention of this will appear on your records, including going AWOL. Not something to be encouraged.

"Not a word to anyone. It never happened. Unthinkable. Dismissed."

Thomas saluted and turned to go, but Keilty remained at attention.

"What about Laird?"

The Governor and Thomas froze at Keilty's tone and the lack of the respectful "sir".

Hastings gathered himself.

"In view of the death of your friends, Yeoman Warder Keilty, I will overlook your lack of manners."

Keilty waited.

The Governor hesitated. His voice was soft with irony.

"Lord Laird died in a hunting accident."

Hastings flicked a newspaper at Keilty.

"You can read his obituary. It's in *The Times* today."

Keilty saluted and turned out of the room without glancing at the paper. Thomas followed him out.

In the Tower Courtyard, it was business as usual. A crowd of school children and their teachers were gathered around a yeoman warder. Keilty smiled at them. He stood on a small step.

"Now, the Tower of London has had its fair share of rascals and rogues. Villains of the highest order."

He studied their rapt faces and it warmed him.

"But perhaps the greatest rogue of them all was Colonel Blood. Does anyone know what he did?"

Keilty scanned the crowd of small faces. As he did so, his eyes rose and he spied General Hastings eyeing him darkly from his narrow turret window.

The world stood still for Keilty. Somewhere in another part of the Tower of London, someone was playing *Greensleeves*. Keilty could hear Tommy Battle laughing, too.

Blinkin' shoot me, Ged. We did it.

Keilty fixed on Governor Hastings, who was still watching him.

Keilty turned away to face his audience. Some arms were raised, waiting to tell him about Colonel Blood.

"Many of you will have heard of him, stealing the Crown Jewels from King Charles II. But I'm not going to tell you about him, I'm going to tell you another darker tale of the Tower. Yes, it features Colonel Blood, but you won't read this in any of your history books at school."

Keilty started to speak. As he did so, one of the young children at the back was writing furiously, trying to keep up with Keilty's tale, despite his sore fingers.

Epilogue

Glengoyne, Scotland, 1926

A man was standing near the summit of a steep hill. From here he could see the castle. He turned scanning the horizon, a walking staff in his hand. He looked in the direction of a small croft. A woman was splitting logs in the yard. It was Karen Gordon. Her hair hung loose. She stopped and waved to him, shielding her eyes from the sun.

He waved back and began to walk towards her.

The ghillie flicked a coin in the air. The sunlight caught it. It landed in his palm. It was a golden doubloon.

McDonald, now with a healthy beard, continued his descent, whistling *Bonnie, Bonnie Scotland* as he picked his way down.

He had travelled the world, fought in the heat and the dust. Dragged his wife, Elaine, from one barren fort to another. Now, she was gone, and that life with it.

He and Karen had both lost people, her to the Great War; him to many wars.

He strode down the hill to a new life.

Karen waited for him. His future waited for him.

He was a man at peace. McDonald had come home.

Mac and Skinstad fight

LONDON, ENGLAND, 1930

The fog seemed to magnify the sound of the footsteps of the man ahead.

Evan Thomas could tell which way his quarry turned from the echo of his boots down the narrow alleyways.

Thomas was conscious of his own steps.

However, the man on his tail was quieter. Well-trained. A professional.

Thomas tried to keep his pace steady. Ahead, the footsteps stopped.

After counting 22 paces, Thomas found his man. He had been dead for less than 20 seconds. There was no sight or sound of his killer. Just a small wooden-handled dagger stuck in his chest. *He must have walked on to it.*

A slight movement behind him and Thomas realised he had company. A well-built, blunt-featured man. He and Thomas considered each other, as the stranger's arm came up. Thomas acknowledged the silenced pistol and braced himself for the bullet.

"Not good odds," murmured the assassin, as he took half a step forward, then another. Thomas frowned as the man in front of him sank to his knees. He folded awkwardly, as Keilty extracted his blade from the man's back.

Keilty and Thomas stared down at the two dead men.

"Jack was right," Keilty's voice was soft as he wiped his knife.

"We have a problem, Ged."

Keilty deftly slid his weapon away. The movement was so

fluid it was difficult to figure out where the knife had gone.
"Mac?"
"Mac. If he's willing…"

Acknowledgements

There are many people who have given their time, advice and support to make this book possible. It would have been much harder without them. In fact, it might not have happened at all.

The list should probably be longer than this, but here goes....

My love and heartfelt gratitude to my family, Douglas and Rosemary Jackson for travelling with me on the journey, who together with Lesley and Danny, have put up with me being stuck in 1925 for years, as well as for their constant encouragement.

Special thanks go also to Leo Callaghan for believing in this story. Thanks also to his talented cousin Matthew Gooder for taking up the challenge and to my dear friends Nigel and Katie for all their patience and support – from Hull and back.

For having faith in this forgotten piece of history, many thanks to Jesper Ericsson, Chris Henry, Dougie Irvine, Sara Harkins and Denise Taylor.

Also to the late James T Duthie, Henry Duthie MBE, Paul Main and The Mannie Glennie, Anne Reid, Stefan Dickers and The Gentle Author, Saskia Gibbon, Don Coutts and Bruce the Navigator, also Richard Findlay, Laurie McMahon, Davie McDonald and the original Ged Keilty.

Not forgetting the Gibson family, Brem and Brenda Bing.

My gratitude and appreciation to Lynne Forsyth for her editing skills, artist Mary May for her stunning cover, publisher Jeremy Thompson and his team at Matador, word whiz Julie Beedie and creative Jonathan McKay. Their help and advice on all aspects of production pointed the way.

Finally, for their expertise and enthusiasm, I salute the staff and volunteers at The Gordon Highlanders Museum, The Tower of London and The Royal Hospital Chelsea. They are inspirational.

Thanks to you as well, for helping me get this far.

About the Author

Mark Jackson is a BAFTA Scotland nominated writer and an award winning short filmmaker; a sometime journalist, photographer and one-time restaurant manager. He was born in England and lives in Scotland, where he works for a small charity.

He can be contacted at:
drumgoynecastle@gmail.com

Tommy Battle